M574s

DEMCO

THE SUMMER I LEARNED ABOUT LIFE

THE SUMMER I LEARNED ABOUT LIFE

CAROLYN MEYER

A Margaret K. McElderry Book

Atheneum   *1983*   *New York*

Library of Congress Cataloging in Publication Data

Meyer, Carolyn.
The summer I learned about life.
"A Margaret K. McElderry book."
Summary: More interested in learning about Life
than domestic arts, as her parents wish, fifteen-year-old
Teddie learns perhaps a bit more about
life than she's bargained
for during the summer of 1928.
I. Title.
PZ7.M5685Su 1983 [Fic] 83–6390
ISBN 0–689–50285–0

Copyright © 1983 by Carolyn Meyer
Published simultaneously in Canada by
McClelland & Stewart, Ltd.
Composed by Service Typesetters
Austin, Texas
Manufactured by Fairfield Graphics
Fairfield, Pennsylvania
Designed by Christine Kettner
First Edition

To Harold, my only cousin and good friend

Table of Contents

THE
SUMMER
I LEARNED
ABOUT
LIFE

1

The Birthday of the Next Amelia Earhart

Fifteen tiny flames jittered on my birthday cake. I hovered over them and rummaged for a wish, something worth wishing for that stood at least a chance of coming true. Then I thought of my brother Rob, due home in the next few days, and huffed out the candles. Magically he appeared in the doorway of the dining room, a smiling genie with a suitcase in each hand and a cardboard box crooked under his elbow.

"Happy birthday, dear Teddie," he sang. I hollered "Rob!" and raced around the dining room table and lunged at him, knocking the box out from under his arm.

"Teddie," Momma murmured, and my sister Hannah said, "Eleanor!" in a shocked voice. Somebody, probably Hannah's husband Will Farquhar, said, "Tsk, tsk."

My family was concerned that I was not growing up to be a lady, and lessons—which I had so far resisted—were to begin seriously that summer. It was 1928, and I wanted to learn about *life*. I was pretty sure that was not what they planned to teach me about.

Rob set down his suitcases and greeted everyone around the table, one at a time.

Poppa half rose to shake hands, his white napkin flapping from the waistband of his trousers. "Son," he said.

"Father," Rob replied.

Next he kissed the cheek Hannah offered him and patted Billy, Hannah's baby, who pounded on the tray of his high chair with his spoon and grinned up at the new face.

Will stood up and stuck his hand out like a lever. Rob worked it up and down a couple of times. "Good to see you, Robert," Will said in the sonorous voice he was cultivating and sat down again.

Momma, beaming at the foot of the table, let him squeeze her. "You look great, Momma," he said. He and I still called her Momma, although Hannah had been calling her Mother for years.

Grace Bissell squirmed in the chair next to mine. Grace was not a member of the family, but almost. She lived next door, was in my class at school, attended the same church and Sunday School we did, and was therefore my best friend, although we had different ideas on most things. Grace also happened to be deeply and secretly in love with Rob. The passion was completely hopeless for two obvious reasons: One, Rob was twenty-one, six years older than Grace, and he probably still thought of her as a child like me. Two, the trip from which he had just come back was a visit to his sweetheart, Peg, in Pittsburgh. Momma and Hannah expected him to announce his engagement any day now. But Grace still hoped.

She shoved her chair back awkwardly, bumping into the buffet, and stood up the way Poppa and Will had, hand out. But Rob ignored the hand, grabbed her around the waist, and planted a loud kiss on her cheek. Grace turned the color of a geranium and sat down quickly. She hitched in her chair and studied the tablecloth in front of her.

He got around to me. "Well, Birthday Girl, let's have a look at you," he said, holding me at arm's length, presumably to see if there were any changes since Easter.

There weren't. I still was short and not fat but *thick*. Momma called it "solid" or "sturdy." My bobbed brown hair would not curl, and it wouldn't lie flat either. Everyone said my blue eyes were my best feature, but I was not allowed to pluck the thick eyebrows that grew too close together. The bridge of my nose was too wide. I had pretty much abandoned all hope of ever being beautiful.

"I perceive," said Rob, scrutinizing me carefully,

"that you are *older*."

Will dragged up an extra chair and pushed it into the space between me and Grace, who busily shuffled her fork and spoon and water glass down toward Momma. Hannah set a place, and Momma loaded a plate with slabs of roast beef, well done the way Poppa liked it, mashed potatoes, and lima beans, and dribbled gravy over the whole thing. We all watched while Rob worked his way through the food, the birthday party suspended until he caught up. I settled down to rolling pink birthday candle wax into gray pellets.

"Tell us about Pittsburgh," Momma said.

"Tell us about *Peg*," corrected Hannah, which I knew was a knife wound in Grace's heart.

"Pittsburgh's a mess, as usual. Even out where the Baldwins live, the air is full of soot." Rob buttered one of Momma's fresh rolls. "Saw some people from school," he continued between mouthfuls, "went out dancing, had a couple of picnics." He wiped his mouth carefully. "A nice time was had by all."

Not a word about Peg. Hannah opened her mouth and closed it again. She turned her attention to me. "Eleanor, you're making a mess with those candles." (She was the only one in the family who called me Eleanor.) "Why don't you serve the cake?"

Two layers of devil's food lurked beneath a lather of white frosting decorated with pink rosebuds. I cut a piece for each of us, Momma scooped strawberry ice cream out of the freezer bucket, and we passed the plates around. Grace had polished hers off before I half finished mine.

"You want another piece, Grace?" Of course she said yes, even though she knew chocolate was bad for her skin. Grace had very little self-control in these matters.

Rob said, "I'll have another piece, too, just to keep you company, Grace." She would hang her dreams on that one remark for at least a week.

"Time for presents," Momma said, after she and Hannah had cleared the table. The gifts were stacked on the buffet behind me. Now this should have been the good part, but to tell the truth, I wasn't looking forward to it. In our family, you didn't necessarily get what you *wanted* but what somebody decided you *needed*.

Momma gave me a Fanny Farmer cookbook and a blue-and-white checked apron decorated with a cross-stitch design. Hannah gave me a pair of white gloves with small pearl buttons and a book called *Etiquette*, by Emily Post, in which I would learn when to take off and put on the white goves.

Poppa, believing that being well-read in the classics was as much the mark of a young lady as wearing white gloves, presented me with a copy of *Gulliver's Travels*, which would now take its place on the bookshelf in my room next to *Robinson Crusoe*, *Tom Sawyer*, *The House of Seven Gables*, and *Wuthering Heights*. He also gave me a small leatherbound account book in which I was to keep track of my income and expenditures because every woman needed to learn how to handle household money.

Will's present was *A Devotional Guide for Young Ladies,* with a daily schedule of Bible readings and prayers. My brother-in-law was studying to be a minister, and he was concerned with my spiritual life, which he guessed—correctly—to be not especially good. He and Hannah and Billy were living with us until Will graduated from seminary and found a church that wanted him to be its preacher. My sister Hannah was going to be a perfect preacher's wife. She would teach the smallest children and sing in the choir and belong to the ladies' guild, and she would produce perfect cakes for bake sales and church suppers, and her house would be immaculate and always ready to receive the people who came to see her husband for spiritual guidance. I could not imagine asking Will for spiritual guidance, but I suppose that was mostly because I wasn't a very religious person and not just because I thought Will was a stuffed shirt.

I was afraid that Grace, attempting to imitate our Family Tradition, would also give me a book. Probably poems by Edna St. Vincent Millay, whose work she was crazy about.

Inside a big square box decorated with bluebirds trailing Happy Birthday streamers was a smaller box in the same wrapping, and so on through four boxes. "To heighten suspense," Grace explained. The last package was indeed the size of a small book, but in it was a red velvet case, hinged along one side. A little brass plate on the front was engraved with my initials and the date, June 8, 1928. I flicked open the case. Inside were spaces for two portraits. Framed in an oval of red velvet and gilt was a snapshot of my dog, Tinny, a good old mutt with black spots and one ear that fell over his eyes. Opposite Tinny was a photograph, clipped from a magazine, of Charles A. Lindbergh.

I kept the secret of Grace's love for my brother, and she kept the secret that I was nuts about the famous aviator. I had read all about Lindy's nonstop flight from New York to Paris on May 21, 1927, and pasted pictures of him and the *Spirit of St. Louis* in a scrapbook. I didn't care that he was twenty-six, since I was not planning to marry him, so the age difference didn't matter. My feeling for Lindy was on a totally different plane (bad pun, but true). I didn't want to be a wife, to Lindy or anybody else. I wanted to be an aviatrix, making my own daring flights across the Atlantic, maybe even around the world. I wanted to share the adventures of the skies with someone like Charles Lindbergh. I didn't want a husband; I wanted a copilot.

What I had really hoped for for my birthday was a sheepskin-lined leather jacket, warm enough for an open cockpit, and a wristwatch with a built-in compass. I had not bothered to mention this to my family since they did not take me seriously. Grace *did* take my ambition seriously and didn't laugh.

Grace dreamed about romance and marriage, and I didn't laugh at her either. That's what made us friends.

Grace grinned, pleased with herself, and I grinned back.

"What a pretty picture frame," Momma said when I passed the velvet case around the table. "Swell snapshot of Tinny," Poppa said. Nobody mentioned Charles A. Lindbergh.

"Hold the phone," Rob said. "I've got something for you too." He set the cardboard box I had knocked out of his arm in front of me. It was not fancily wrapped like the other presents, but the inside was stuffed with wads of squashed newspaper, which I carefully extracted. The tip of a propeller emerged first, and then the tail. I dug faster and lifted out a tissue-thin paper and balsa-wood model of Lindbergh's airplane, the *Spirit of St. Louis*.

The name was painted on the silver nose, *N-X-211* lettered under the wing, and *RYAN NYP* on the tail. I spun the propeller and ran the wheels over the palm of my hand. "It's wonderful," I said. "Thank you!"

"What does NYP mean?" Grace asked, reaching up to stroke the silvery body.

"New York to Paris," I said. "Ryan was the company that built it." There was hardly anything I didn't know about Lindbergh.

"Did you see the card?" Rob asked.

" 'To the next Amelia Earhart,' " I read. Maybe

Rob actually took me seriously, too!

"Who is Amelia Earhart?" Momma asked.

"A flier," Rob explained. "An aviatrix who is taking off sometime this month on a plane from Newfoundland to Wales. She'll be the first woman to fly the Atlantic, if they make it. Two men and Amelia."

"I can't imagine such a thing," Momma said. "Land sakes. Why would a girl want to do anything like that?"

"She probably couldn't find a husband." Hannah sniffed. "Do you know how old she is?"

"I think I read that she's thirty," I said.

"An old maid," Hannah said firmly.

"Isn't it time for some singing?" Poppa asked, rising from his chair. The birthday party was over.

"Ahhh, sweet mystery of life, at last I've found yoooou!" Poppa bellowed, completely off key. Singing was part of Schneider Family Tradition, and it was usually Poppa who suggested it. We had a Victrola and a large collection of records, mostly operetta music. He also liked grand opera, especially Wagner, and on Sunday afternoons in the winter he sat by the radio, as if it were a religious ceremony, and listened to the sopranos howling up at the Metropolitan Opera House in New York City. Nobody else in the family liked opera.

Poppa wanted us children to play musical instruments. Hannah had studied violin and was so talented that she won a scholarship to a conservatory, but she turned it down and married Will instead.

Rob had scraped away on the cello for a few years, but he hated it and when he was thirteen, he quit his lessons and taught himself to play the ukulele. The cello was in the attic, next to Hannah's violin. Rob had a terrific voice, and he could read music or hear a song on the radio a couple of times and play it right off the bat.

By the time I was old enough to begin music lessons we had gotten a piano, and every week I was sent first to Miss Culbertson and then to Frances Keeler, when she began to teach. Her family and ours had been friends for years, and she had been Rob's high school sweetheart. Frances did her best to teach me to play. So had Miss Culberston. I had less talent than Hannah and Rob, but I was pretty good at hymns, as long as they had no more than three flats or two sharps. I could play most of the other songs the family liked to sing, too.

Hannah and Momma did the dishes, excusing me from the chores on account of my birthday. Will carried Billy into the living room and settled into a wing chair with the baby on his lap. Poppa eased into a matching wing chair and folded his hands over his sloping stomach. Grace's offer to help with the dishes was refused, and she maneuvered so she could be next to Rob on the davenport. I wondered if he ever noticed what she was up to. I went to the piano.

Poppa said, "Why don't you girls sing something?"

and Grace and I launched into our duet, "Whispering Hope," which we always sang at the drop of a hat. Next we all ripped through "Give of Your Best to the Master," and a few others, Rob singing bass and Will faking the tenor, because he couldn't read music as well as he thought he could.

Momma came in from the kitchen, patting wisps of hair back into her bun. "It's wonderful to hear all of you making such a joyful noise unto the Lord."

" 'Oh sing unto the Lord a new song; sing unto the Lord all the earth,' " Poppa said, stroking his stomach.

" 'Sing unto the Lord with the harp; with the harp and the voice of a psalm,' " Will countered, leaning toward Poppa with a satisfied smile. Will was always trying to show Poppa that he knew more about the Bible than Poppa did, which he didn't.

Hannah put Billy to bed, and we sang more hymns, and then I said, "Rob, it's your turn," and waited for him to get his ukulele.

"No," Rob said. "Not today."

Rob rarely refused, and I spun around on the piano stool and stared at him.

"You must be tired," Momma said soothingly. "Why don't you go have a nice hot bath?" Momma believed that a hot bath was a cure for almost everything.

"I think I will. That train was filthy. Happy Birthday, Teddie." He winked at me and smiled, but the smile was peculiar. Grace noticed it, too.

"He didn't mention Peg once," she whispered. Exactly what I had been thinking. Grace looked almost pleased. I couldn't blame her, but it made me mad anyway.

Before I went to bed, while Poppa was winding the clocks and Momma was locking up downstairs, I knocked on Rob's door. He was at his desk in his pajamas and bathrobe, writing something. "Sit down, young lady," he said, and I perched on the edge of his bed. "Did you have a nice birthday?"

"Yes. Did you have a nice trip?"

"Yes."

"Really?"

"Could have been better." He screwed the top back on his fountain pen.

"So could my birthday."

"How?"

"If I tell you, will you tell me about your trip?"

"Probably not."

"Why not?"

"Because I'm your big brother and you're my little sister and it's none of your business. I think of you as a little girl, y'know, even if you're turning out to be a gorgeous dame."

I blushed and said, "Ha."

"Why 'ha'?"

"If only! If only I were either still a little girl and could play with dolls and stuff, or else a gorgeous dame out flying my airplane! But I'm stuck here in the middle, and all anybody in the family can think about is making me into a Perfect Woman. *Their* idea of a Perfect Woman, anyway."

"What's wrong with that?"

"Because it's not what I want to be! It's what Hannah is. She was a Perfect Girl who wanted to be a Perfect Woman, get married, and become a mother and have Perfect Children. That's not what I want."

"I still don't see what's wrong with it."

"For one thing, I might end up married to somebody like Will."

Rob laughed. "Not your type, huh? Will's not so bad when he's not playing preacher." Rob tipped back in his chair. "So tell me what's on your mind."

"This Perfect Woman business. Being able to make flaky piecrusts and gravy without lumps and put sheets on the bed so tight you could bounce a nickel on them. The Perfect Woman can't have any ideas that other people think are odd, like wanting to be a flier. She has to think what her husband thinks." I could have rattled off a list as long as my arm about what was expected of me, now that I was fifteen.

The difference between sons and daughters was that sons weren't expected to be *truly* perfect, the way girls were. That's one reason I was glad Rob had come home for the summer. I hoped that he'd understand and help me get out of this ridiculous training program, this rehearsal for a part I didn't want to play.

"It isn't what I want to be learning," I said. "Ironing shirts and darning socks and stuff."

"What *do* you want to be learning? Automobile mechanics? Bricklaying?"

"I want to learn about *life*."

"Life? Like what?"

"Oh—you know—the things that happen to you whether you want them to or not, plus all the things that you *wish* would happen, plus the things you're *afraid* are going to happen, and why they happen that way, and how to get the good things and not the bad ones."

"That's a tall order, Teddie. I can't teach you about those things. Nobody can. You just have to learn about life by living it, I'm afraid. Anyway, I'm the last person you should be asking. And what bad things can happen to you? You're going to marry some nice guy and live happily ever after, just wait and see."

"That's one of the things I'm afraid of. Maybe I don't want that. But how do I know what I want if I don't know about *life*?"

Rob sighed, stood up, and stretched. "Teddie, you think too much. And I'm too tired to answer your questions now. Even if I had the answers, which I don't. Why don't you talk to Momma?"

So I said good night and went to my room. What

do you do when everybody you know looks at things the same way, including the *one* person you had counted on? Momma, of course, was exactly the person *not* to ask. She would not have understood that I didn't want to be like her. Grace and I had had a few dead-end conversations on the subject, and she couldn't see what I was talking about either. Her views were very narrow. She aspired to Perfect Womanhood, like Hannah.

And then I remembered the way Rob had looked when we asked him to sing, and that he still hadn't said a word about Peg. Maybe *he* was learning about life, but he wasn't passing any of it on to me.

2

What I Learned in Three Days

The circle of dough stuck to the rolling pin and ripped when I tried to flip it over. I pinched it together with my fingers and dusted on more flour. Hannah saw me, naturally.

"It's going to be a very tough crust," she said.

This was my fourth lesson in piecrusts, and she expected me to do better.

"There are certain things every housewife has to know how to do," Momma had said, "and then there are things it's just *nice* to know how to do." Pies, she felt, were somewhere in between. The object for today was lemon meringue.

While the crust browned in the oven, I went to work on the filling and meringue. I've watched my sister whip egg whites into a cloud that floated on the surface of pie like fog and came out of the oven a high, tender puff, but the blanket of meringue I spread over the lumpy filling shrank and toughened like wool in hot water. I set this inept creation on the windowsill to cool. Grace came in and stared at it.

"I think it looks fine," she comforted. "My mother won't even let me try. She's always afraid I'll make a mess. Besides, you're getting *paid* for it."

The fact that I was earning money made it easier to bear. Momma had thought of the scheme and proposed it to Poppa. He agreed that I would be paid on a piecework basis, once I reached an "acceptable level of competence," to be determined by Momma and Hannah. Hannah disapproved of the idea because housewives don't get paid for their work, except in satisfaction. Momma set up a schedule—a nickel for an ironed shirt, ten cents for a pie or cake, and so on—and tacked it to the cellar door. I would collect my wages on Saturdays.

"It's not exactly making me rich," I told Grace. "That pie is incompetent and unacceptable. It won't earn me a red cent."

"It's a knack," Momma assured me, coming up from the cellar with a wicker basket full of wet clothes. "You'll catch on. Now, why don't you hang out Rob's clothes and then fix yourselves a nice glass of lemonade."

Happy to be handling anything that belonged to Rob, Grace shook out each shirt and pair of pants, and I pinned them to the clothesline.

"How does he like his job?" Grace asked.

"Fine, I guess. It's filthy work, but he says he doesn't mind because the pay is good."

Rob had gone to work for the telephone company in Philadelphia, fifteen miles away, crawling down manholes to trace the underground cable system. He earned twenty-five dollars a week and was saving most of it for college in the fall.

"I saw him polishing the car on Sunday," Grace said.

"Yes, he loves to work on that car."

"My father says he shouldn't be doing that kind of work on Sunday," Grace said. " 'Remember the Sabbath day to keep it holy.' "

"But it's not *work* for Rob. He likes doing it. I don't think that's violating the Sabbath at all." Mr. Bissell, Grace's father, often had something critical to say, and her mother was even worse. Somehow Grace was a nice person who hardly ever said anything bad about anybody.

"If you like doing it, then it's not really work, is that right?"

"That's right," I said, although I wasn't sure. Grace was always trying to get me into discussions like this. I propped the clothes pole under the sagging line, and we went inside to make lemonade.

"What about Peg?" Grace wanted to know. We took our glasses to the front porch. "Has he said anything?"

"Everything's fine," I lied. "They had a wonderful time. You might as well just give up on this, Grace," I advised heartlessly.

Grace slumped in the wicker rocker. "I suppose they'll be announcing their engagement soon." She sounded tragic.

"I suppose so."

Dramatic sigh. "I guess I'll go home, Teddie."

"Okay. I have to go set the table anyway."

The men began coming out from the city about five-thirty. They walked up our street from the train depot, tugging at the knots of their ties and loosening their starched collars—except for Rob, who came home in dirty work clothes. Rob's first stop was the hall table, where Momma had left the mail. Twice a week there was a square white envelope with tall, back-slanted handwriting and a Pittsburgh postmark. Rob would grab the envelope, race up the stairs two at a time, and shut his door.

Will arrived next, easing his tie only when he was safely inside the house. That summer he was an assistant pastor at a big church in Philadelphia, and he always wore a black suit and looked miserably hot and proud of it.

Last came Poppa, slapping the evening newspaper against his leg, calling out good-evening to our neighbors. Occasionally he and Grace's father, a red-faced man with wobbling jowls, walked home together. I supposed Poppa was nice to him because of the commandment to love thy neighbor. Poppa's arrival was the signal to put dinner on the table.

We took turns saying grace at meals. Momma and Hannah and I always said the same prayer. Will made up a new one each time, something elaborate. Poppa did Sundays, adding a long list of things we were to be thankful for, in addition to the food. And Rob *sang* the blessing when it was his turn. "Praise God from whom all blessings flow," he'd begin and we'd all join in, always making it seem like a special occasion.

Our meals were standard—no experiments, nothing out of the ordinary—because Poppa didn't like surprises. Chicken on Sundays, roasts on birthdays, turkey or ham on holidays, chops and cheap cuts during the week. Conversation was generally limited to "Please pass the salt," or Momma coaxing us to have another spoonful of this or that. Sometimes Rob described what he and Otis, his partner in the manholes, had seen that day. Then came the dessert, formerly made by Hannah, the highlight of the meal until I began my lessons.

Momma carried in the lemon meringue pie, sawed through the cardboard crust, and passed out flat triangles that leaked lumpy yellow goo. Nobody said a word, but I knew there would be no dime for that one.

"Ironing," Momma said the next day, "is a necessity. Nobody but your own family knows if your cake falls, but the whole world sees if your husband's shirts aren't done right."

I didn't mind hanging up and taking down and folding clothes, but I hated ironing—especially shirts and blouses, which had to be starched.

"Start with the collar, Teddie dear," Momma said. "Then the cuffs. And when you do the front, check the buttons. Men have a fit if one's missing."

While I slaved over a pile of shirts, Grace folded a pile of Billy's diapers, which she loved doing. Grace adored babies. It was ironic that I was getting the lessons for being a housewife, which I did not intend to be, and Grace, who was obsessed with the idea of getting married and having children, was not being taught anything at home. Whatever she knew, she learned by watching me.

Grace also wanted to be a poetess. She worshiped Edna St. Vincent Millay and Rupert Brooke, an English poet who had died a tragic early death in the world war. Grace read that he had been handsome, charming, and dashing. He reminded her of my brother Rob.

"If only Rupert hadn't died young," she'd lament. "I'd marry him in a minute."

"He'd be old enough to be your father," I'd remind her.

Grace finished the diapers and perched on a kitchen stool to read to me. " 'The heart once broken is a heart no more/ And is absolved from all a heart must be.' That's Millay. Doesn't it make you want to *weep*?"

"This collar is making me weep," I said. "How can anybody actually wear something like this?"

"I don't know. I'm just glad I don't have to. Here, I'll read you a sonnet I'm working on. 'I love thee in the morning of the springtime,' " she intoned from her notebook, " 'I love thee in the afternoon of fall./ But when the stars shine in thine eyes of winter/ I love thy summer heart the best of all.' There. That's the first stanza. How do you like it so far?"

"Ummm," I said. "But what's all the 'thee' and 'thine' stuff? Why can't you just say 'you' and 'your'?"

"Because it's poetry," Grace said. "Because I like the sound of it."

"Maybe so, but how about the people you're writing it for? Maybe they'd prefer something more like the way they really talk. 'I love *you* in the morning of the springtime.' But it's very pretty, really, Grace," I hurried on when I saw the hurt look pinch up her face.

Grace could not stand to have her poetry criticized, and I don't know why she bothered to read it to me. If I offered suggestions, she got hurt feelings, and when I said it was nice or pretty or something, she said I wasn't being honest.

"*Why* do you think it's pretty?" she demanded.

"Because it rhymes," I said. "I like the rhymes."

"That's no reason," she said impatiently. "Of course it rhymes. That's like saying you like the sky because it's blue. The sky *is* blue. Poetry *does* rhyme."

"Not all poetry does," I argued, heaven knows why. "Blank verse just has meter. Da *dum* da *dum* da *dum* da *dum*." We had studied meter in English class in the morning of the springtime.

"That's not real poetry," she said fiercely. "I don't care what Miss Sprankle says. Edna St. Vincent Millay's poems rhyme. Rupert Brooke's poems rhyme."

"Okay, Grace." I never read poetry unless I had to. Maybe if Grace had written poems about Lindbergh or Earhart, I'd have been more interested. But she did promise to compose a poem in honor of my first solo flight.

"Eleanor, you're scorching that shirt!"

Hannah, coming to fix Billy's lunch, pointed to the iron-shaped brown mark on the yoke of Poppa's shirt.

"Uh-oh." There went another nickel.

"You really have to keep your mind on your work," Hannah scolded. "You're always off in the skies somewhere."

My sister strongly disapproved of my plans to be an aviatrix. If for some reason a woman could not find a husband or was widowed or struck by some other disaster, then she should be a nurse or teach young children. Anything else was unnatural, she said. Dreaming of being a flier was absurd, ridiculous, childish, and worst of all, unladylike. Hannah used to think it was cute when I talked about flying, until she realized I meant it. A minister of a church could not possibly have a sister-in-law who flew airplanes.

"Grace," I said, working on another shirt after Hannah had gone out to the backyard with something disgusting to feed Billy, "when are you going to have time to write poetry with children to take care of? The ironing and cooking and all."

She smiled dreamily. "I'll write stories for them in verse form," she said. "Like nursery rhymes and Mother Goose songs and things like that, for bedtime. And sometimes after dinner we'll sit around the fire and the children will make up songs and poems, too. It will be a family activity."

"You'll be too exhausted," I said. "I've been standing over this ironing board for two hours now, and I certainly don't feel like writing anything."

I put the ironed shirt on a hanger and buttoned every other button. Poppa's and Rob's shirts hung in their closets; Will, however, insisted that his be folded in a certain way and stacked in his drawer in rotating order. Hannah did them.

"This is the kind of thing," I told Grace, "that a wife has to learn about her husband in order to please him. How much cream he likes in his coffee, which part of the chicken he likes best, how wide he wants the window opened at night. Hannah says it's all part of a wife's duty."

"I think it would be a privilege, not a duty," Grace said piously. "Don't you ever wonder how Lindy wants his shirts done or whether he prefers the drumstick or the white meat?"

"Probably the wing. You know—so he can fly better?"

"Ha ha."

Next in the basket was a stack of Rob's work pants and shirts and a tumble of union suits and pajamas.

"Grace," I said cagily, "how would you like to iron some of Rob's clothes?"

"Oh, Teddie, would you let me?"

"You can start with his pajamas," I said. "I'll show you how."

Which is how I learned to get the ironing done.

But the next day I learned something that had nothing at all to do wth housework.

After breakfast I scrubbed the pot with the oatmeal burned to the bottom and took the dirty clothes down to the cellar. While I was turning the pockets inside out, I found something in Rob's trousers—a little gray, cloth-covered notebook—and flipped it open. In Rob's handwriting, small and neat as needlepoint, I began to read, "I, Henry Robert Schneider, Jr., have decided to keep a diary. . . ." It was dated June 11, two weeks ago, right after he had come home.

There was a brief battle between curiosity and

respect for privacy. Honor won out and I stuck the notebook in my skirt pocket. I'd put it in his room later.

We always took an hour or so off after lunch. Momma went upstairs to prop up her feet which swelled in hot weather. Hannah sewed in her and Will's room while Billy took his nap. Grace had gone somewhere with her mother. I should have been reading *Gulliver's Travels*, but I didn't feel like it. I sprawled on my bed and stared up at the *Spirit of St. Louis*, hanging by a string from the ceiling light. What must it be like to sit in the cockpit of a real plane like that, the roar of the motor filling your ears and the whole world spread out below? Free, I thought.

Then I remembered Rob's notebook, still in my pocket.

It was wrong to look into it. A diary is a private thing, and reading someone's private thoughts is a kind of stealing. But I yielded to temptation. I decided I would just *glance* at it. Rob wouldn't mind at all. If I asked him, he'd probably even tell me to go ahead and read it.

So I read it, and this is what I learned about someone else's life:

Tuesday, June 11. I, Henry Robert Schneider, Jr., have decided to keep a diary, someplace to pour out my feelings. Because it seems that pouring them out to Peg is no use at all. Sometimes I think she doesn't have the slightest understanding of who I am. Peg is a peach, the most beautiful girl in the world. She's been wearing my fraternity pin for six months and I hope she'll announce our engagement soon, even though it's years before we can think of marrying. But I'll feel an awful lot better when the engagement is made formal. When I told her last week that I feel engaged already, she just smiled and said, "Let's wait and see." Now what does *that* mean?

Saturday, June 15. I was talking to Otis about Peg, telling him that she's a *real* beauty because she looks as good first thing in the morning as she does when she's dressed up to go out in the evening, and he picked up on that "first thing in the a.m." part and leered. I knew what the leer meant, but I've never done anything at all with Peg. She's too nice a girl for that. I firmly believe that sex should be saved for marriage, no matter how strong the temptation. I suspect Otis doesn't share my views.

Wednesday, June 19. Every day Otis asks me, Hear from Peg? More than half the time the answer is no, and even when it's yes I feel rotten because the letters aren't the kind I want. She doesn't seem to like to write. Days go by with nothing, and then comes a single page. She always sounds so impersonal. She doesn't say that she misses me or that she loves me. Every day I rush home looking for a letter, and when there is one, it drives me crazy. I write to her every night, sometimes filling up three pages, telling her how much I love her, that she's the dearest thing in all the world to me. But she never replies to any of that. It's as if I never said it.

Saturday, June 22. Otis says it's a big mistake to write so often to Peg, that I ought to get dates with other girls. But I'm trying to prove that I can be true to her, that I'm worthy of her. I'm just going to work hard and write to Peg every night to show her how much I cherish her. Maybe that way I'll win her, and she'll agree to announce our engagement.

Sunday, June 23. Warren Jennings came over last night and talked me into going to Willow Grove to listen to a dance band. I never should have gone. Every song the band played made me yearn for Peg. I felt so blue I could hardly stand it. When I got home I wrote out the lyrics of our song, "Always," to send to her like a poem: "I'll be loving you, Always/ With a love that's true, Always." Maybe that will make her understand how much she means to me.

Those are the highlights. I skipped over the parts about Otis's philosophy and stuff about work and other things I wasn't interested in. When I shut the book and put it on Rob's desk, nothing terrible happened—lightning didn't strike me dead, there was no mighty clap of thunder. But now I knew things I didn't want to know. And once you've stolen someone's private thoughts, there's no way you can give them back or get rid of them, no matter how much you want to.

3

Being Good But Not Too Good

Henry Robert Schneider, Jr., was not the only one who needed a place to pour out his feelings. So did yours truly, Eleanor Louise Schneider. I decided if Rob could pour it out to a diary, so could I.

I had to ask Momma for the money, since I had not yet managed to save enough nickels and dimes from my wages.

She was lying down with her puffy feet on a pillow. I told her I needed a quarter, and she said, "Help yourself." Notice that she didn't ask me what I wanted a quarter for. She never did.

Privacy was a basic part of the Schneider Family Tradition. I don't mean the ordinary kind of privacy, like closing your bedroom door. I mean the *other* kind, like not talking about what you were feeling. You were expected to keep such things to yourself.

Grace's family was different. Her mother was an eavesdropper. Once when Grace and I were in her bedroom talking, I tiptoed over and jerked the door open and caught Mrs. Bissell pretending to be putting something into the linen closet next to Grace's room. If Grace got a letter from somebody, a cousin for instance, Mrs. Bissell was waiting for her with milk and cookies and a thousand questions about everything that had happened. No detail was too inconsequential.

It was a relief to walk into my own house after a dose of Mrs. Bissell and have Momma ask, "How was your day, dear?" and I'd say, "Fine," even if it hadn't been really, and she'd say, "That's nice," and that would be the end of it. Once in a while I wished she'd ask more questions. But it was better than Mrs. Bissell's constant searching into every corner of your mind as though it were a room that had to be cleaned.

If Momma had found Rob's diary, she would have known that it was private, and she would have laid it on his dresser and not even *wondered* what was inside. Hannah would not have looked at it either, or cared.

Well, that was the difference; I *did* care. I bought a notebook like Rob's, but with a blue cover, and began to write down my observations, beginning with what I knew about Rob:

1. Handsome—tall, wavy brown hair, nice blue eyes, lopsided smile.

2. Talented—wonderful singer, ukulele player, dancer, actor; plays leading roles in dramas that glue you to your seat and in musical comedies that make you laugh and hum.

3. Popular—liked by everybody, little kids, old ladies; high school senior class voted him "Most Likely to Succeed."

4. Happy—or was, until Peg Baldwin came along. Now just another role he's playing, a mask he wears. Behind the happy mask is the True Rob, whom I discovered in the diary.

Maybe, I thought, everyone wears a mask that covers the True Person underneath. Which brought up the question of the True Me, whoever *that* was. One part of the True Me I hoped no one would ever unmask was the one that had gotten into Rob's diary and discovered the True Rob, who undoubtedly didn't want to be discovered.

Even though I felt guilty, I was going to keep reading it, either until things got better or until I could figure out a way to fix them. Originally I just wanted to know what was going on, what it was like to be in love and planning a future together. I may have had strange ideas about some things, but I still believed in love, a least for other people.

After I had begun reading Rob's diary and keeping my own, family dinners were not the same. Now

I had to be alert for clues—not only to the True Rob but to the True Everyobdy Else as well. I kept my nose bent over my plate and listened. If we were having an unusually talkative meal, for the Schneiders, conversation might go like this:

"Billy got a new tooth," Hannah would report.

"Bless his heart, how many is that now?" Momma would ask.

"Eight. You know who I saw today at the market? Frances Keeler."

"Oh, and how's Frances?"

"Just fine. I told her she must come by and visit."

"Mamie, have you heard from Ida?" This was Poppa. "Are they coming for the Fourth?"

"Yes, and bringing Marybelle's beau, Earl."

"The one who looks like a sausage?" Rob would chime in.

"Hush, that's not nice! Yes, that's the one."

"What's new in the manholes, Rob?"

"It's awful. Otis and I are supposed to take turns going down to check the cables, while the other one reads the survey maps, but somehow he always works it out so he's up on the street, clean and dry, and I'm the one who has to crawl down the ladder into those slimy holes."

"More meat loaf, anybody? Scalloped potatoes?"

"What's for dessert?"

"Cupcakes with chocolate icing."

"Think I'll save room for one. How did they turn out today, Teddie?"

"They look strange, but I think they'll taste all right."

And so on.

I'm not sure what other families talk about. Probably nobody comes out and says, "My girl friend doesn't love me and I feel terrible," in front of everyone. Nobody would know what to say, except "More meat loaf?"

Rob's diary got to be the most important thing in my day. I knew I shouldn't, but I kept on reading it, and that in itself got to be tricky because he carried it to work with him in his pants pocket. It was just accidental that he had forgotten it that one time. After that I had to devise ways to get a chance to read it.

Then another letter came from Peg. Momma propped it against the vase of peonies on the hall table, and I stared at it off and on all day. I tried holding the envelope up to the sunlight, but her stationery was so thick that nothing filtered through. I had heard that it was possible to steam letters open, but I was afraid to try. And that seemed to be going too far.

Rob came home, seized the letter, and raced upstairs with it as though it were a winning sweepstakes ticket. His bedroom door closed. Much later, water gushed into the tub and a long time after that he came downstairs, freshly shaved, his hair slick, his eyes red-rimmed and hollow. "What triumphant masterpiece, what chef d'oeuvre is in store for the lucky diners tonight, Teddie?"

It was baked custard that had turned watery, as a matter of fact, but I was bothered by the way he looked and sounded. His joke didn't come off. Sarcasm didn't suit him. Nobody else seemed to notice.

It was my turn to say the blessing, but my mouth was dry. "Don't mumble, Eleanor," Hannah said. "Speak clearly and loudly enough so everyone can hear. It's not a private prayer."

"Just because you can tell me how to bake pies and stuff," I said to Hannah, speaking clearly and loudly enough so everyone could hear, "doesn't mean you can tell me how I'm supposed to pray."

"Teddie!" Momma said, shocked.

"Teddie, that was uncalled for. Apologize to your sister," Poppa ordered.

"I'm sorry for the way I said it, but not for saying it, because it happens to be true."

"That will be *enough*, Teddie!"

The platters and bowls went around, and I stared at the slab of swiss steak, which I disliked, and four Brussels sprouts, piled like cannonballs, which I detested.

Then Rob suddenly launched into a story about the pump wagon that came to empty out the manholes after a heavy downpour had filled them with rainwater.

"The one good part," Rob said, "was the old geezer who operates the pumper. He swears like a sailor. I've never heard such a colorful vocabulary. Every other word is a curse word."

Momma clucked, "Tch, tch." No one else had anything to say. That was the end of the conversation.
I still had three Brussels sprouts on my plate and
nine-tenths of the steak.

It wasn't the kind of story that anybody but me
was interested in. Nobody in our house—including
Rob—used bad language out loud. He would not
have told a story like this, which he knew the family
wouldn't appreciate, if he hadn't been upset about
something, and I might not have noticed if I hadn't
discovered the True Rob.

I had to wait a whole day to find out what had
happened. He came home at noon on Saturday and
took Momma out shopping. While Poppa was weed-
ing the vegetable garden and Hannah and Will had
taken Billy out visiting, I crept stealthily into Rob's
room. The diary was on his desk. Open.

"Damn it all to hell and back!" my non-swearing
brother had written. "It was another one of her
don't-give-a-damn letters, saying she's decided to
write no more than once a week. She thinks I
ought to go out on dates. Then she ends with 'Be
good but not too good.' Very nice and considerate
of her. She wants to have dates, so she tells me to
go out too so she won't have a guilty conscience.
She can go out and have a good time if she wants
to, I'll be damned if I'll stop her. My first thought
was to write and tell her what I think of her con-

stancy, but I'm not going to give her that satisfaction. I'll stop writing for a while just to show that two can play this game. She says I mustn't get upset, we should just have a good time and not take everything so seriously, but my God, I'm human! I get so mad at her sometimes I see red, and yet I can't keep a lump out of my throat. I've looked to her for love, encouragement, and devotion, and she's given me indifference, discouragement, and unfaithfulness. A hell of a life this is!''

"Grace," I said, "will you please give me your definition of poetic justice?"

We were playing Chinese checkers on Grace's bed.

"Poetic justice is when somebody gets what's coming to him in some ironically appropriate way."

"Just desserts, would you say? Comeuppance?"

"Yes. Why? What are you talking about?"

"I'm not at liberty to say just now. But let's suppose there's this person who is not treating this other person the way the second person deserves to be treated. The second person always treats the first person very well, but the first person treats the second person very shabbily. And I think you'd agree, if I could tell you the full set of circumstances, that this shabby-acting first person deserves a comeuppance. Just desserts. Poetic justice is what's called for."

Grace rolled a marble in her hand for a few seconds and then made an amazing series of jumps across the board and right into the point of my star. "She's giving him the brush-off, eh?"

I lurched on the bed, the springs sang, the marbles rolled. "What are *you* talking about?"

"Same thing you are. Peg's breaking his heart, and you want to get even, right?" She collected a marble that had wandered under the bed. Grace could be terribly irritating.

"How did you know?"

"Intuition." She shrugged. "I'm a poet, and poets are sensitive and intuitive, that's all. How did *you* know?"

"He let it slip," I lied.

"But Teddie, how do you plan to give her her just desserts?"

"It's obvious," I said. "Rob falls in love with somebody else and writes to Peg and tells her he'll always treasure their friendship but, alas, he has found his true love."

"That sounds good, but where are you going to find somebody for him to fall in love with?"

"I don't think it *really* has to happen. Peg just has to *think* it has."

"And how are you going to do that?"

I had no idea. For a while neither of us said anything. I was busy thinking rationally and Grace was busy intuiting. Usually she got there first, but this time I beat her to the punch.

"This is pretty old hat," I said, "and it might not

even work, but it could be worth a try. Suppose we got some compromising photographs of Rob and sent them to Peg? Anonymously, of course."

"Now where on earth are we going to get compromising photographs of Rob?"

"Well, we could borrow your father's camera and take some."

"Of whom?"

"I was thinking maybe of you."

"Teddie, just what is it you're asking me to *do*?" she demanded in a voice that sounded almost like her mother's.

"Grace, I wouldn't ask you to do anything I wouldn't do. Besides, you've been crazy about Rob for years, since you were twelve. It won't kill you to spend a few minutes pretending to be his true love."

The board was set up for another game. I made the first move and explained my plan. "You and your parents will be over at our house for the Fourth of July as usual. I'll have some money saved for film. We'll start singing, the way we always do. And you can just sort of sidle up to Rob and put your arm around his shoulder or something and—"

"And you'll be snapping pictures and catch us *in flagrante delicto*." Grace loved to use Latin phrases. I knew what that meant: in the very act, red-handed.

"Yes, I guess that's it. Will you do it, Grace?"

"I'll sacrifice myself. I'll try to make myself look older, or at least enough older so that when Peg sees the pictures she won't be able to guess that I'm only fifteen."

"Thank you, Grace," I said. "I really appreciate this. It's for a good cause."

"I'm doing it for Rob."

Fireworks for the Fourth

I smeared white polish on my shoes in honor of our country's 152nd birthday, and then Grace and I went downtown to watch the Fourth of July parade with our friend, Julia Gibbs. The best part was the pet division, lots of kids leading dogs dressed in costumes or hauling cats in wagons with signs like DANGEROUS WILD TIGER and BEWARE OF THE BEAST.

"You should have brought Tinny," Julia said. "Dressed him up in a sailor suit or something."

I had, in fact, once put him in a clown outfit and a pointed hat with a red pompom. I wore a hat to match and painted red circles on my cheeks. We won third prize and my face broke out in a rash. I would never do such a thing now, at the age of fifteen.

After the parade we bought ice cream cones and walked over to the schoolyard. Grace and I hitched ourselves up on the brick wall and helped Julia scramble up next to us. She was worried about messing up her pale-yellow dress.

Julia was outstandingly the prettiest girl in our class, with shining golden hair and light brown eyes. She had nicer clothes than anyone, too, and she was always perfectly groomed. Boys swarmed to her like bees to honey, but she didn't seem to care about that. Julia took piano lessons and voice lessons and dancing lessons and was being tutored privately in French because her mother thought she was not acquiring the proper accent in class. Once a week she received an elocution lesson to learn how to round her vowels and crisp her consonants. She passed it all on to us: "Around the rough and rugged rock the ragged ruffian ran," she mouthed, and we imitated her until we collapsed laughing.

Julia was being prepared by her mother for a Good Marriage, which meant a husband with money and prestige—foreign royalty, maybe. The amazing thing was that in spite of everything her mother did that would have turned practically anybody else into a real pain, Julia remained a good friend. In fact, instead of envying her, we felt a little sorry for her.

"What are you two doing this summer?" Julia asked us. We didn't see much of each other after school was out, because Julia lived on the other side of town.

"Studying domestic arts," I said. "Rolling out pie-crusts and starching up shirts and darning socks. I'll begin knitting and crocheting when the weather turns cool." In a Good Marriage, Julia wouldn't have any use for such practical stuff. There would be servants.

Grace sat hunched over with her chin almost down on her knees, tracing designs in the dust with a long stick. "Poetry," she said, "is what I'm doing. And observing life."

The three of us had been acquainted for years, but we had not become friends until I discovered Julia crying her eyes out in the girls' bathroom at school after she had sung an operatic piece in the weekly chapel program. "I made a mess of it," she had wailed, although she hadn't. Somehow seeing her with puffy eyes and a running nose like any other mortal made it possible to be friends. I believe her mother would have preferred that she not associate with social inferiors like us, but in our school there wasn't much choice. Nobody knew what Mr. Gibbs would have preferred, because he had deserted them when Julia was a child. We ate lunch together at school every day. Grace and I brought our bologna sandwiches in a brown paper bag; Julia's lunch was packed in a little wicker basket with a cloth napkin and real silverware fitted inside the lid.

Julia was one of the few people who knew that I wanted to be an aviatrix.

"You should get a special flying costume," she

advised, licking around the edges of her cone. "Like Harriet Quimby's plum-colored flying suit."

"That satin suit didn't keep her from falling out of her airplane when she was flying upside down over Boston Harbor," I reminded her. I had almost finished my cone.

"Are you going to be a stunt flier?" Grace asked, sounding worried.

"No. I'm not a daredevil, Grace. I just want to fly around the world."

"And that's not being a daredevil?"

"Well, a little, maybe."

Grace talked about poetry and romance, I talked about airplanes and flying, and Julia talked about her passion: horses. Julia claimed that she didn't care about a Good Marriage; that was strictly her mother's dream. *Her* dream was to live in the country and raise horses.

While we were talking, some boys that we all knew came by, and they flirted with Julia and acted the fool for her benefit and ignored Grace and me. Julia played her part and flirted back and laughed at their antics, but not too much, and when they had gone, she told us her news.

"I'm finally taking riding lessons," she said. And I love it. It's much better than dancing lessons and French and all of that." A large drop of chocolate ice cream had fallen on her skirt, and she scrubbed at the stain with a lace-trimmed handkerchief.

Her mother had bought her boots and jodhpurs

and a red jacket and a shirt with an ascot, she told us, and twice a week she went out to the stables in Fairmount Park and took lessons on a chestnut gelding named Blaze.

"There's more," she said, and her gold-flecked eyes glowed. "A secret." We crossed our hearts with our eyes closed, our old ritual. "His name is Tommy O'Connor, and he works in the stables. He's Irish, of course, and he even talks with a brogue. And he's so handsome!" He had taught her how to saddle Blaze and brush him down after the lesson and reward him with a bucket of oats. Her mother didn't know about the extra instruction. "I'd die if she found out about Tommy," Julia said.

"How old is he?" Grace wanted to know, always concerned about age differences.

"Twenty-three."

"Twenty-*three*! Why Julia, that's much too old!"

"I don't think so," Julia said dreamily. "It just makes him *mature*. He's such a kind and serious person, not at all kidding and crazy like the boys at school. And it's wonderful to see him with the horses. You should see the way he touches them."

"You haven't let him touch you, have you?" Grace asked bluntly. Grace was not one to beat around the bush.

"Of course not," Julia said, but she didn't look at us when she said it. "But please, you must keep your promise not to tell anyone, because if my mother finds out she'll make me stop the lessons, and it's the only thing I've ever really enjoyed."

I had a piercing moment of doubt. Grace was my best friend—closer than Julia because of living next door—but I would not have told Grace anything that absolutely had to be a secret. Grace told her mother everything, not even meaning to, sometimes not even realizing what she doing until it was too late. Mrs. Bissell believed it was her duty as a parent to know exactly what Grace was doing, thinking, and feeling, and she pried it out of her, wheedling over the afternoon snack, until Grace caved in. And once Mrs. Bissell knew, that was *it*. If Grace spilled the beans, her mother would instantly inform Mrs. Gibbs of every detail, and that would be the end of Julia's riding lessons and of Tommy O'Connor.

"The thing is," Julia said, "I'm in love. Look." She pulled a fine gold chain with a heart-shaped locket up from inside her dress and opened it carefully. There was no picture in it, just a dark wad of something. "A lock of Tommy's hair," she whispered reverently, letting us look before she closed the locket and dropped it out of sight again inside her dress.

"When do you see him?" Grace whispered, although there was no one in sight.

"Tuesdays and Thursdays. I just live from one lesson to the next. And we have so little time together, only what we can manage while I have my lesson and groom the horse afterwards. If I'm too late getting home, that would ruin it. We're hoping that somehow we can manage to see each other more. I don't know how, but Tommy's working on a plan."

"What kind of a plan, Julia?" Grace asked. I wished there were some way to stop Julia from answering. But there was no way.

"Oh, listen, you two! I'm so excited I could burst. Tommy wants me to marry him!"

Grace and I gasped. Julia flushed a pretty pink and covered her face with her perfectly manicured hands.

"You wouldn't do anything like that, would you?" Grace demanded, not whispering now.

"Oh, I don't know, I don't know!" Julia keened. "I keep telling him I'm too young, we'd be stopped, he'd be arrested, it would be awful. But he says we'll keep it a secret until I'm old enough, and then nobody can keep us apart."

"That's two years from now," I said. Julia had had rheumatic fever when she was little and had been kept back a year in school, so she was already sixteen, a year older than we were.

"A year and a half, Teddie. I'll be seventeen on January first. But promise me, promise me you won't tell a soul!" We crossed our hearts a third time.

We were walking slowly toward the corner where Julia would catch the streetcar to the other side of town when I had a bright idea. "Would you like to come to my house for a picnic this afternoon? We have plenty of food and everybody would be glad to see you again. Rob can drive you home afterward."

"What a nice idea. I'd love to, but I want to go home first and change. I've got this spot on my dress." The dribble of ice cream was barely visible. "And I have to ask my mother. I'll see you in a couple of hours, if it's all right."

The trolley clanged along the track, Julia climbed aboard and waved to us, and it rattled off with her. Grace and I started home, passing remnants of the parade.

"Did you get some film for the camera?" Grace asked.

"All set. Maybe we could get some pictures of Julia, too," I suggested cautiously. "Some of Julia and Rob together, maybe."

Grace looked at me sharply. "You've decided Julia would be better in a compromising photograph than I would, haven't you?"

"Well, wouldn't it be better to have a couple of pictures?" I hedged. "And Julia is older. It's for the good of the *cause*, Grace. If we're going to achieve poetic justice and give Peg her just desserts for what she's doing to Rob, then we have to be willing to make sacrifices for the comeuppance, don't you agree?"

"It's okay, Teddie. I understand."

But I knew I had hurt her feelings.

When I got home Rob had already been to the train depot to fetch the first batch of relatives: Uncle

Luther, Poppa's brother, his wife, Aunt Ida, and Cousin Marybelle and her beau, Earl. Marybelle was a tall, bucktoothed girl with as much shape and style as a telephone pole, and Earl was shorter by a couple of inches and definitely on the chubby side. Furthermore, he wore his clothes a size too small. He was so stuffed and buttoned that he *did* look like a sausage, ready to burst if he took a deep breath. Earl and Marybelle had just announced their engagement, and she was showing off a glittering speck on her left hand.

They were planning a Christmas wedding, and Aunt Ida could not stop talking about all the things that had to be done in the next five and a half months. In a week, for instance, Marybelle would be sitting for her engagement portrait.

"The reception will be at the Warwick," Aunt Ida burbled.

"In the city? Isn't that a long way for everybody to travel?" Momma asked. We had had Hannah's reception in the social hall in the church basement, a damp and gloomy place even with candles and flowers on all the tables.

"Well, Mamie, it just seems that since Marybelle here is our only child, we want to do it up right. Don't we, Luther? And Marybelle has had her heart set on this for a long time. Right, sweetheart? We're going to have a tea dance," she continued, "with a string ensemble."

Marybelle flashed us a toothy smile and squeezed Earl's pudgy hand.

"You're going to have dancing?" Rob asked, suddenly coming to life. "I want to dance every waltz with you, Marybelle," he said gallantly, "even if it makes Earl as jealous as all get out. I might even chase away the violinist and sit in with my ukulele."

"Oh, Rob, you wouldn't dare," Marybelle squealed.

"Better not try it with my bride, old fellow," Earl warned with a fake-sounding chuckle.

There was a flurry as Aunt Rebecca, Poppa's sister, and Uncle Albert drove up in their Ford with my younger cousins Emily, Ferd, and Dickie. At the same time Julia arrived, dolled up in a peppermint-striped dress and a straw hat with a pink ribbon. The arrival of the newcomers gave Aunt Ida an excuse to start all over again on the wedding plans. Meanwhile, Momma and Hannah and I were galloping back and forth to the kitchen, bringing out tons of food. Julia wanted to help, and I put my birthday apron around her and prayed that she wouldn't mess up this dress too.

When we had all the bowls of potato salad and deviled eggs and so on set out on the table in the backyard, Poppa began to carve the ham, and the Bissells made their appearance. Grace had piled her hair on top of her head, propping it up with combs, and she was wearing one of her mother's blouses with

a brooch planted squarely in the middle of her bosom—all, I guessed, designed to make her look older.
It worked. She looked old enough to be her mother's
sister.

Mr. and Mrs. Bissell shook hands with my aunts
and uncles and said silly things to my little cousins
and congratulated the newly engaged couple. At that
moment Julia emerged from the kitchen with a
pitcher of iced tea in each hand. I saw Mrs. Bissell's
mouth drop open and then snap shut again and an
expression cross her face as though she had just swallowed a fly. Oh-oh, I thought; here comes trouble.

Poppa asked the blessing and we all helped ourselves. The food reminded Aunt Ida of the menu
for the wedding reception. "Smoked turkey and Vir-
ginia ham and lobster Newburg in little patty shells,"
she said, cutting our ordinary ham into tiny pieces.

Grace sat on the porch steps with her father's camera in her lap. The idea of the compromising photograph that had seemed so good in Grace's bedroom
a few days ago was now looking pretty dumb. How
would Rob look compromised with somebody practically middle-aged? But it was *Rob* who said, "Hey,
Grace, are you going to take pictures?"

Grace got to her feet as though rheumatism had
already settled into her bones and shoved the combs
deeper into her topknot. "First the future bride and
groom," she said, and when they had snuggled up
together and giggled and composed themselves for

the camera, she snapped the shutter. Next she lined up the three young cousins with Tinny sprawled on Ferd's lap.

"Okay, now you, Teddie," she announced, but I hated to have my picture taken and ducked away. "How about Rob and Julia?" They obliged, stiffly facing Grace and the camera. "No, move closer," Grace instructed. They obeyed, but still she wasn't satisfied. "Rob, why don't you just put your arm around Julia?" Rob looked puzzled, but he did it, and Grace finally took the picture.

"Grace, how about if I take one of you and Rob?" I said.

"Fine," she said. "But I've got an idea! Let's play a game, sort of follow-the-leader. Julia will play, won't you?"

I had never heard Grace so full of false enthusiasm. I was going to have to take her aside and have a little talk, but before I could think how to maneuver that, she plunked the camera in my hands and flung her arms around Rob's neck. I was so surprised —but not as surprised as Rob was—that I almost didn't snap the picture. Her hair tumbled out of its precarious bun and two combs dropped to the ground. She looked wonderfully helter-skelter.

"Your turn, Julia!" Grace cried. Julia, self-possessed as always, stepped up to Rob, who was better prepared this time, and placed a demure kiss on his cheek. I recorded the moment on film.

"Well, say!" Rob exclaimed. "It's not every day

that I have two beautiful women paying me a compliment like that!" He collected Grace under one arm and Julia under the other, and all three mugged for the camera.

"Got what you wanted?" Grace muttered under her breath, stooping to retrieve the combs.

"That was just terrific, Grace," I said, still amazed at her.

"I did it for the cause," she said coolly. "Because I *care*."

We finished off the roll of film, and then Aunt Rebecca and Uncle Albert decided it was time to take Emily, Ferd, and Dickie home because they were beginning to sass, and they offered to drive Julia back home at the same time, if she didn't mind piling into the backseat on somebody's lap. Marybelle and Earl announced that they were going for a stroll.

That bunch gone, the womenfolk settled down in the lawn chairs for another glass of iced tea, some of Hannah's cookies, and a chat. The men—Rob, Poppa, Uncle Luther, Mr. Bissell—chose up sides to pitch quoits.

Mrs. Bissell had worked her way over next to Aunt Ida. "It must be very gratifying," Mrs. Bissell said in that whiny voice of hers that made me shudder, "to have a daughter starting off her married life, and with such a fine young man." I don't know how she knew Earl was a fine young man. I thought he was kind of dull. "You never know about some people," she said, and dropped her voice to a raspy whisper. "Now would you ever in all your life suspect for one minute what that lovely creature Julia has been up to? That she is on the brink of *ruin*, if not already there? And is positively breaking her dear mother's heart?"

I shot a murderous look at Grace, who was searching the grass for four-leaf clovers. You'd better come up with one in a hurry, I thought; you're going to need all the help you can get, Grace Bissell, if you've done what I think you've done.

"It was all I could do to be civil to her, the little floozy," Mrs. Bissell was saying. "I've heard that Julia Gibbs, that perfect princess, has gotten involved with a stable boy. Imagine that!" She reared back, smacking the arms of the lawn chair.

All right, Grace, you're going to get it. I don't care if you did pose for a compromising photograph with my brother.

"A stable boy?" Momma asked in her mild way. "If he's a good Christian, then that's all that matters, isn't it?"

"He's Irish and Catholic, Mamie," she announced grimly, "and twenty-three years old."

"Oh dear," said Momma. "That does shed a different light on the matter, doesn't it?"

You really did let the cat out of the bag, didn't you, Grace, I thought. I could guess exactly how it went. Her mother waiting for her to come home, sitting at the kitchen table with a cup of coffee in front of her, nothing to do because they were coming here for supper and anyway her mother hates to cook. Her mother probably said something like "Tell me about the parade," and Grace went on about the baton twirlers and the pet parade. And then Mrs. Bissell asked, "Did you see any of your other friends?"

"Julia Gibbs was there," she would have replied.

"Such a lovely girl! So refined! She has everything, doesn't she? Beauty, intelligence, talent, and she's so *sweet*. What a blessing to her poor mother. How *is* Julia?"

At that point, overcome by jealousy, Grace probably blabbed. Bit by bit by bit. And Mrs. Bissell could be counted on to tell Mrs. Gibbs tomorrow, at the very latest, if she hadn't told her already.

"Come into the kitchen with me for a minute, Grace," I said sternly. Grace hauled herself up off the clover patch and followed me, her head hanging over her mother's brooch. "Damn you, Grace!" I said when the screen door thumped behind us.

"Teddie! That's swearing."

"I know it's swearing. I don't give a damn. You betrayed her! You broke your promise and told. And *now* think what's going to happen!"

Grace started to bawl. "Ma just dug it out of me. I wasn't going to tell her, honest I wasn't, but she just kept *at* me and *at* me—you know the way she does—and I finally couldn't keep it in any longer."

There was no use pointing out to Grace that she

could have held out if she really wanted to. You just couldn't trust Grace.

Somebody in the backyard started singing "In the Evening by the Moonlight," and then Rob came into the kitchen and looked surprised to see us standing there.

"Getting your uke, Rob?" I asked him.

He shook his head. "I've had enough romantic stuff for one day. Anyhow I've got to write a letter."

Marybelle and Earl, back from their stroll, were getting the folks in the backyard to sing "Let Me Call You Sweetheart," and Rob went slowly upstairs to his room. The singers were right under his window. I knew that he would be writing to Peg, his heart breaking when he heard that song. Julia's heart was also probably breaking, or would be soon, on the other side of town. I leaned against the sink and glared at Grace, who was noisily blowing her nose, and I felt that our friendship was going to pieces, too.

5

The Wrong Side

Grace and I sat on the front porch, not speaking. She slumped in a creaky wicker rocking chair and sketched flower designs in the margins of her poetry notebook. I struggled with a soggy piece of embroidery, a pillowslip on which I was working the outline of an airplane with *Spirit of St. Louis* in script below it.

The wrong side of needlework always shows how good you are, Momma said. Hers was as neat on the back as it was on the front, while mine was a tangle of knots and loops. Just like my life, I thought: looks all right on the surface but a mess underneath.

I knew that Grace was feeling guilty about Julia, and I was feeling hardhearted, figuring she deserved the guilt. I stitched and blotted my sweaty hands.

Grace sketched and sighed. The clock on the mantle bonged three. Even time seemed slowed down by the heat.

I heard running footsteps on the driveway, and suddenly Julia dashed up on the porch, her riding habit wrinkled and her hair churned into a frenzied cloud around her blotchy face. She flung herself onto the settee and sobbed, letting the tears run down her cheeks and drip onto her shirt.

"It's all over!" she cried between sobs. "My mother found out about Tommy!" She snuffled. "Do you have a hanky?"

I didn't, but I handed her the *Spirit of St. Louis* pillowslip. She blew her nose on the end opposite the embroidery hoop. "My life is ruined," she croaked.

Surely, I thought, Julia is going to light into us, to accuse Grace and me of giving away her secret. She would know instantly who was to blame. Grace turned as white as a sheet. Her lips moved but no sound came out.

"I want to die," Julia gasped. "It was that awful Mr. Slawson." She wiped her nose with her hand and fumbled for the pillowslip again.

"Mr. Slawson?" I repeated. Grace just stared.

"Mr. Slawson who owns the stables. He found us together this afternoon in the tack room, and Tommy was kissing me. He fired Tommy right on the spot, told him to pick up his things and get out. Then Mr. Slawson told me if I'd kiss *him* he wouldn't tell my mother what he'd seen. Oh, he's *awful*—a filthy, disgusting monster! I slapped him, good and hard. You could see the red marks on his face. That made him furious. He made me stand there while he called my mother and told her to come and get me. And he said *horrible* things to me. He said he felt sorry for my mother, having a slut like me for a daughter."

Julia dug her fingers into her stormy hair. "When Mother came, he changed completely, making her think he's a perfect gentleman. He told her that he had seen Tommy *fondling* me. He said that he had 'reprimanded that young buck in the past for taking liberties'—those were his exact words—but that he had thought the girls were partly to blame for inviting the advances. He told Mother he was sure I was innocent, and he had sent Tommy away so that his 'burning lust won't defile pure young womanhood.' Oh, that dreadful man, trying to make me think Tommy's a bad person! Tommy *loves* me!" She started to cry again. She was making so much noise I expected Momma or Hannah to come out to see what was going on.

"Mr. Slawson told Mother he'd take over my riding instruction himself, that I'm very talented and he doesn't want to see that talent go to waste. I said no to that. I'm not taking any more riding lessons now. But what difference does it make? Tommy's gone, and I don't know where. Oh, what am I going to do?"

Then Grace started crying, too, and she moved over to the settee and put her arms around Julia. I wasn't used to being around weeping people, and I went into the kitchen to get some cookies for everybody, just to give myself something to do.

"Does your mother know you've come here?" I had a sudden vision of Mrs. Gibbs roaring up onto the porch and the whole ruckus starting all over again.

Julia shook her head. "She sent me to my room," she said, "but I climbed out the window and went down over the porch roof. I guess I tore my jodhpurs," she said, fingering the rip.

"Just the seam," I said. "I can fix that."

We went upstairs. Grace was still not acting right, but Julia was too upset to notice. I loaned her my robe and got out a washcloth and towel. While I mended her pants, Julia tidied herself up.

"Everything is going to be all right," I said, not believing it but hoping it was true. "You'd better go home, though, before you get in worse trouble."

Momma and Hannah would be coming out of their rooms any minute now to start fixing dinner. Grace and I escorted Julia to the corner where the trolley stopped.

"Are you going to try to find Tommy?" Grace whispered.

"That's none of your business, Grace," I said sternly. "Don't tell us if you are," I warned Julia. "We don't want to know."

Julia rubbed her forehead. Her eyes were still a little puffy, but otherwise she looked pretty good.

"It has to be a secret," I went on. "Some things you just have to keep to yourself."

"All right," Julia said. We heard the trolley, and she hugged us both. "Thanks for being my friends."

Grace and I settled back to the silence we had been sharing for a couple of days. After a while Grace said, "It isn't my fault. My mother didn't tell her mother."

"You're lucky. It *could* have been your fault. You have to learn to keep your mouth shut."

"I know."

I was anxious to get home. I knew they'd be waiting for me. But Grace was walking slower and slower.

"Do you suppose," she said, speaking slowly, too, "that Julia ever let Tommy . . . you know, *touch* her or anything?"

"I don't know."

"But don't you kind of wonder?"

"Not much."

"Don't you *ever* wonder about things like that?" Grace asked accusingly. "My mother has been talking to me lately."

"Your mother talks even more than you do."

"You don't have to be nasty, Teddie."

"I'm sorry." I really was in a nasty mood. I couldn't help it. Nothing seemed to be going right. "I guess I do wonder sometimes," I confessed. Actually I wondered a *lot*, but so far my domestic training hadn't included anything about sex. "What else does your mother talk about?"

"She talks about purity. I don't think my mother believes in sex."

"Well, certainly not *now*, Grace," I said, sounding as prissy as an old maid. "Not until you're married."

"I know that. I don't mean *now* either. But I don't think she thinks much of sex even after you're married."

"You must have misunderstood her. After all, sex is necessary for procreation. How else would we be here?"

"It seems there's another kind of sex, though. That it's not just to have a baby. Know what she told me?"

"What?" She had me curious now.

"That it's a wife's duty to submit to her husband, but that a husband who has true respect for his wife will demand that she submit only when he can no longer delay his need for gratification." She squinted at me, waiting to see what I'd say.

"She makes it sound awful."

"Maybe it *is* awful. What do you think?"

"Probably it's awful for women but not for men. Otherwise why the talk about his gratification? She didn't say anything about the husband submitting to the wife's need, did she?"

"No. I guess women do it just to have a baby."

"My mother never said if it's good *or* bad. She just says young girls should keep their minds on other things, and that there's time enough to discuss it when I'm engaged. But since I'll probably never be engaged, I may never find out what it's all about."

"I wonder how long a man can go before his need for gratification can no longer be delayed. It sounds so terrible that I think once every six months ought to be enough, don't you?" Grace had reason to be worried; she wanted seven children.

"Why don't you ask your mother?"

Grace shook her head. "Oh, I couldn't."

"Why not? She asks you everything, doesn't she? Why can't you ask her something like that?"

But I knew the answer. Mrs. Bissell could barge into Grace's life, but if Grace asked her mother such a question she would have been "disrespectful" or "impertinent."

"Grace," I said, "since I'll probably never be engaged, let alone married, I may never find out what it's about. So will you promise me something? That if you find out some real facts, you'll tell me?"

"Sure, Teddie," she said. "I'd be glad to. But it's possible that you might find out first, and if you do, will you tell *me*?"

So we made a pact to share whatever sexual knowledge came our way, and that's how we ended the bad feelings between us.

I took a stack of dinner plates from the kitchen cupboard and dealt them around the table, doled out the everyday silverware, and laid a linen napkin in a ring next to each place. I set a water glass at the tip of each knife and speculated about my parents and sex. The thought made me so uncomfortable that I shifted the speculation to Hannah and Will.

I had been my sister's junior bridesmaid, dressed in a peach-colored gown that she had made me. After the reception in the gloomy church basement, the bridal party came back to the house. Ruth and Floss, the other bridesmaids, helped her change into her going-away suit for the trip to Niagara Falls. They were fussing and giggling, and they forgot I was there, sitting on the edge of the bed in my bridesmaid's dress.

"Oh, Hannah, isn't this exciting? Tonight you'll find out what it's all about."

"I wish that part was over with," Hannah said.

"But Will's such a gentle person," Floss said. "I'm sure he won't hurt you any more than he has to. And they say after a while you even start to enjoy it."

"Do you hope you'll get pregnant right away?" Ruth asked.

"Hush," Hannah said, catching sight of me in her dressing table mirror. I kept my head down and stroked the satiny folds of the wedding dress she had taken off and was planning to pack away until it was my turn. I was twelve then; the dress would probably rot in the attic before I got around to wearing it.

I was fourteen when Billy was born. Hannah was very weak when Will brought her home from the hospital and carried her upstairs to their room. Momma took care of Billy for a couple of weeks until Hannah was strong enough to be up and walking around.

"Did it hurt when Billy came out of you?" I had asked. She was nursing Billy, his tiny face pushed up against her breast. I think she didn't want me there when he was eating.

"It's all part of being a woman, Eleanor," she said.

I had begun to get my periods a few months before Billy was born and suffered from monthly cramps. Momma's explanation was the same: "It's all part of being a woman."

What were the *good* parts, I wanted to ask, but here was an example of the kind of thing we never discussed in our family.

Rob came home, whistling, while I was in the kitchen cutting biscuits. There was another square envelope with the Pittsburgh postmark propped against the peonies, and the whistling stopped when he saw it. He called hello to us as he dashed upstairs. Pretty soon I heard water running into the tub. He usually spent about twenty minutes in there, and that was my chance to catch up on my snooping.

I told Momma that I had to go to my room for something. So as not to be a liar, I got a handkerchief out of my drawer (which I should have had for Julia and spared the pillowslip) and then sneaked into Rob's room. The notebook, as usual, was in his pants pocket. I heard the water start to gurgle out of the bathtub. Next he'd shave. There was not a chance in a million he'd come out at that moment, wet and dripping. The letter lay on his desk, but I was not tempted to look at it. This was an agreement I had reached with my conscience: I would read his diary but not his letters, proving I had some strength of character and was not like Mrs. Bissell.

I needed only a couple of minutes to skim through the last entry, dated the night before. He described a softball game that I already knew about because Grace and I had been there. Rob wasn't adept at softball, but he was such a good-humored sport that nobody cared. *He* cared, though, even if it was just the Sunday School team. Next he described a movie he had seen with his pal, Warren Jennings. "I'm just crazy about the movies," he wrote. "If I could be anything in the world, I'd be an actor, like Douglas Fairbanks, and I'd be in the movies. But of course Father would never hear of such a thing. I have no choice but to follow his wishes and become an engineer."

So much for my idea that Rob could do whatever he wanted.

I went downstairs again and put the butter on the table and the ice in the water pitcher, and then Momma rang the silver bell on the buffet to signal dinner was ready.

Rob came last to the table, and as soon as he walked into the dining room I was sorry I hadn't broken my rule and read the letter on his desk. It was written all over his face that the world had just fallen in on him. Nobody else seemed to notice. He ate in silence, explained that he was worn out, and went back upstairs before he had even had a dish of chocolate pudding. I had to wait a full twenty-four hours to read what had happened.

"Tuesday, July 9. It's all over. Peg says she's through. She won't wear my pin anymore, we're to be nothing but casual friends. She says she can never forgive me for calling her a failure, and I don't even remember using that word. I've just mailed a letter to her, special delivery, begging forgiveness. She's right, I'm wrong. It has been all my fault. If only she'd let me go out there for a weekend, I'm sure I could win her back.

"I can't get thoughts of suicide entirely out of my mind, but when it comes right down to it, I can't do that. It would be too hard on my family. Furthermore it would be a black mark against Peg's good name, but I honestly don't think I can stand being without her. And so my mind is made up. If Peg is really through with me forever, then I'll not go back to college. Father would never consent to my quitting, so when I leave here in the fall I'll let them think I'm going up to school, but instead I'll go out West somewhere.

"I can't tell anyone, not even Otis or Warren. I think I can get a job doing something, and I'll stay until I've forgotten I ever loved a girl named Peg Baldwin. Now that's all over, and I've got to travel the rough highway of life alone, without the girl I love."

"Teddie?" Momma called from the foot of the stairs. "Don't forget the gravy!"

I swirled flour and water in the roasting pan and thought about what I had read. Suicide. Going out West. I was scared. Should I tell somebody? We might not see him again for a long time. How long does it take to forget somebody you love? Six months? A year?

I imagined what it would be like on Labor Day, when the relatives would be here for a picnic to say good-bye to Rob, thinking he was on his way back to college. Poppa would probably deliver his standard speech:

"Son," he would say, "you have an opportunity to go further in this world than anyone in this family ever has." (And he didn't mean out West.) "But you must take your responsibilities seriously. Your grades last term were not, uh, particularly commendable." (Rob had to take calculus over again.) "I would suggest that you waste less time with the theater group and the fraternity, less time attending to attractive young ladies," (a knife would go through Rob's aching heart) "and settle down to your engineering studies."

Rob would promise solemnly that he would make academic work his highest priority (he always promised that), but he would be lying, because he would already have the train ticket to somewhere in the West. Then he'd kiss us all good-bye, and Momma would cry a little as she always did when he left. He'd get on the train, and instead of changing at Harrisburg for the northbound train to Willardsville, he'd stay on straight through to Chicago and who knew where after that. And what was I going to do about it?

The gravy looked good—rich brown, nice and thick, no lumps—and I poured it into the gravy boat. Momma put the meat loaf, already neatly sliced, in front of Poppa's place, and rang the silver bell. Rob wouldn't leave until Labor Day, still almost two months away. A lot could happen in that time. No need to worry yet.

Rob came in looking like a ghost, except for his wrists, which were coated with pink calamine lotion.

"Poison ivy is driving me crazy," he said. Angry red bubbles shone through the chalky coating. "Must have picked it up at the ball field the other night."

Everyone sympathized. I blessed the food. We all helped ourselves. Poppa drenched everything in gravy. He loved gravy. When he had finished what was on his plate he sometimes had a slice of bread with more gravy.

We began to eat. "What's wrong with this stuff?" Poppa demanded after the first mouthful.

Momma glanced at me. "Is there something the matter, Henry?"

Hannah tasted it. "Sugar instead of salt," she pronounced. "The cook must have been daydreaming again."

We had to throw out all the food on our plates and then start over again, without gravy. I took very small servings because there wasn't much left. What an awful meal.

Rob looked at me once but said nothing. I wondered where he'd go out West. A man with a broken heart would probably go someplace rugged like Colorado or Wyoming or Montana and get a job on a ranch where he'd work so hard and so long that he'd have no time to think and remember. He'd learn to bust broncos and rope steers, and there would be nothing to remind him of the past. Just cowboys and wranglers who rolled their own cigarettes and maybe even chewed tobacco and squatted around the campfire and spit into it.

I could imagine how the family would react when they found out that Rob was not in college but out West roping steers and chewing tobacco. Hannah would take it as a personal insult that he had not told us the truth. Will would be shocked that Rob was doing menial work. Momma would be sad and wistful because Rob was so far away, but she would think he was probably having a nice time and learning a lot. Momma always believed the best of everybody and trusted things to turn out for the best, no matter what.

But Poppa would be sputteringly furious, because

his ambition for his son—to have a college degree—
was lost. Poppa's bad moods made everybody around
him uncomfortable. He would fume about the
weather, the news on the radio, the way the meat was
cooked. Momma never seemed to mind Poppa's
stormy moods. She just smiled and went her own
cheerful way. "He doesn't really mean any of it, you
know, dear," she'd say, but his gloom would hang
over the house like a thick, black cloud. To make it
worse, I was the only one who would know why Rob
had gone.

A lot would depend, I decided, on how the compromising photographs turned out.

6

Peaches

The hood of our car was propped up, and Rob and his friend Warren hung thoughtfully over the engine, like horses at a trough. A set of tools was spread out on a flannel cloth on the sidewalk, and once in a while Warren or Rob would bend down and pick one up. They tinkered and tested, and I tried to see what was happening without getting in the way.

"What are you doing?" I asked.

"Checking the spark plugs," Rob said.

"What does a spark plug do?"

"Ignites the gas."

"Isn't that dangerous? Why doesn't the whole thing blow up?"

"Not exactly the gas," Warren corrected. "A vaporized mixture of gas and air." He looked up at me from under his ginger-colored eyebrows. "What's all this sudden interest in the internal combustion engine? I thought girls your age were occupied with clothes and hairdos." He went back to tinkering.

"She wants to fly airplanes someday," Rob explained. "So she needs to know about engines and things like that."

"Fly airplanes? I'll be darned." Warren wiped his greasy hands on the rag that hung out of his back pocket. "Another Amelia Earhart, eh? Interesting." He studied me as though he had never seen me before, as though I were a visitor from a distant continent, and then went back to work on the engine. But he left a space for me to stand where I could watch them.

Warren was Rob's best friend the way Grace was my best friend. They had known each other for years, and when they were in high school Warren used to spend as much time at our house as he did at his own. I was used to the sight of his enormous feet sticking out from under the car. Warren was a whiz at anything mechanical. When Rob went away to college, Warren went to work for a camera shop. He fixed cameras and worked in the darkroom, and he talked about having his own shop some day.

I liked Warren, I guess, but I never could get used to his teasing—that is, I was never sure when he was teasing and when he wasn't. For instance, at that minute I wasn't sure whether he actually believed I would be a flier some day, or if he really did think I should have been interested mainly in clothes.

After they had gotten the engine tuned up the way they wanted it—"Smooth as silk," Warren said with satisfaction—they washed the car and then let me polish it with a chamois while they sprawled on the grass under the elm tree. It was hard work, but I rubbed it until it shone like a dark sapphire.

Warren stayed for dinner. There was never any problem of what to do with leftovers when Warren ate with us; there weren't any. He had a huge appetite, and Momma loved to feed him. After the dishes were done I went out to the backyard to watch Rob and Warren and Poppa and Will pitch quoits. Grace came over and sat beside me on the steps. The humidity had taken the curl out of her hair, and she had large dark circles of perspiration under her arms. I got a whiff of perfume before she even sat down. Something like honeysuckle gone crazy.

"Do you like it?"

"Well, it's really powerful, isn't it?" I like honeysuckle, but I hate perfume. I wouldn't be caught dead wearing it.

Grace hugged her knees. "Yeah, I think I put on too much."

In a matter of seconds the mosquitoes were attacking like vultures. She swatted. I swatted.

When the game ended, Warren came over and sat next to us. If he smelled the honeysuckle, he didn't say anything. "I almost forgot, Teddie," he said. "I

brought your pictures with me. Two of each, right?"
He handed me the yellow envelope with the compromising photographs.

"How did they come out?"

"Pretty good. You'll see for yourself. Must have
been quite the wild party you had here. I'm sorry I
couldn't make it."

Grace and I got some milk and cupcakes and took
them up to my room so we could study the pictures.

"Hurry up, Teddie. Let's see them." Patience was
not one of Grace's virtues.

I spread them out on my bed, one at a time, moving the shots of Tinny and the little cousins off to
one side and concentrating on the compromising
photographs.

"Perfect," I said.

"Julia looks pretty good, too."

"No better than you. You look like a real vamp."

"I do? Do you really think so?"

"Yes."

"What are you going to do with them, Teddie?"

"Send them to Peg, of course. That was the whole
idea, wasn't it?"

"Are you just going to stick them in an envelope
and mail them anonymously or *what*?"

"I don't know. I'll figure something out."

We nibbled our cupcakes, up from the bottom,
saving the icing for last.

"I wonder how Julia's doing," I said, looking at
the picture of her. "Maybe we should have invited

her over to cheer her up."

It was a dirty dig in a way. I knew Grace was still suffering guilt because she had told her mother about Julia and Tommy, and even if she had not been the cause of Tommy being sent away, she *could* have been. The reason I mentioned Julia was to remind Grace of what had happened, in case she decided to let her mother know about the compromising photographs.

"Julia is probably doing the same thing we're doing," Grace said. "Sitting in her room and wondering what to do with herself. I know that I did wrong, Teddie," she said, "and I'm sorry about it. I'm going to try hard to keep my mouth shut from now on, even though you know how my mother is. In fact, I'm making a vow not to tell her things. But it doesn't help if you keep making me feel bad about it."

"I'm sorry, Grace. I want to help you keep your vow."

I really was sorry, and I really did want to help her. Compared to my sin of snooping, Grace's sin of blabbing wasn't that awful. But I still didn't quite trust her.

It got too dark to pitch quoits, and we heard the men saying good night to each other. Grace slowly finished the last cupcake and went home. "See you tomorrow," she said.

I put on my nightgown and got out my blue-covered notebook. I hadn't been very good about making entries, but now I had something that *had* to be written down. I was making a vow, too: never to read Rob's diary ever again.

I had been doing a lot of praying lately, without the help of Will's *Devotional Guide for Young Ladies*. (The young ladies for whom that book was written obviously never had any of the problems I did.) My Sunday School teacher, a sweet-faced lady who always wore an old-fashioned hat with a veil, had told us that we should concentrate on prayers of praise and thanksgiving and stop asking God for things. "Pestering" was her word for it. Frivolous requests were a nuisance to God, and if you annoyed Him by asking, you were pretty sure not to get what you asked for—like birthday presents: you got what you *should have*, not what you *wanted*.

I had discussed this proposition with Grace, who agreed with our teacher but then confessed that she prayed for signs.

"Signs?"

"Well, if I'm trying to make up my mind about something, and I can't, I ask God to send me a sign to let me know what I should do."

"For instance?"

"If I don't know whether to practice my piano lesson or study geometry, I ask for a sign—if there's an even number of cookies left in the jar, that means I have to do math."

"And you think *God* determines how many cookies are in the jar? Odd or even? And that's His message for you?"

"Well, it's not always that simple, Teddie. You asked for an example. But yes—God does everything. Even cookies."

I was sure that would be considered frivolous. I would not pray for a sign, but I was not against making a bargain.

I addressed God: "Please help Rob. Don't let him be so miserable that he goes out West." I thought of adding, "Please let Peg love him so he'll be happy," but I didn't know about that. Maybe that was asking too much.

My part of the bargain was the vow, and I wrote in the notebook, "I, Eleanor Louise Schneider, do solemnly promise that I will not read the diary of my brother, Henry Robert Schneider, Jr., no matter what. Thereto I set my seal this—" What date was it anyway?

The calendar hanging above the telephone on the stair landing had all twelve months on it, so you could stand there on the eleventh of July (which is what it was) and see exactly what date in September Labor Day would fall on and figure from that when it would be time to go back to school. Rob used this calendar to mark the passing of the summer. He circled the date he had come home (my birthday) and the date he would leave, and each day he drew a diagonal line through that square. So far he had marked off a month plus one week. He had one month plus three weeks to go, which meant I had one month plus three weeks to resist temptation. It seemed a good idea at this point to pray for strength, too.

I still had no idea what I was actually going to do with those compromising photographs. The one of Rob being hugged by Grace, the combs flying out of her hair, was good. So was the one of Julia. Grace looked wanton, not middle-aged; Julia looked demure. Which would make Peg more jealous—wanton or demure? I decided on one, then the other. Annoyed at myself, I tossed them up in the air. When they fluttered down on my bedspread, they both landed right side up. A sign, if I ever saw one.

I took a sheet of light blue paper and an envelope from my desk drawer, printed BEING GOOD BUT NOT TOO GOOD across the sheet, wrapped it around the two snapshots, addressed the envelope to Miss Margaret Baldwin, borrowed a stamp from Momma's desk, and dropped the envelope in the mailbox on the corner before I lost my nerve or changed my mind.

The light was still on in Grace's bedroom when I came back from the mailbox. I gave the quiet "yoo hoo" that was our signal, and Grace's head appeared in silhouette at the window.

"I mailed both of them," I said softly. "Cross your fingers and say a prayer that jealousy will bring her back."

"Slow down!" Poppa said.

Rob eased off the throttle. We poked along for a few minutes, and then gradually he fed it more gas.

"Don't go so fast! Your mother gets scared."

Once again the car slowed to a crawl. Momma was serenely watching the scenery unwind past her window, her hands relaxed in her lap. But Poppa was always very nervous in the car. He anchored himself to the strap by the window.

The speed increased almost imperceptibly, but Poppa perceived it and exploded. "Where in blazes is the fire?" he roared.

Poppa was a terrible driver, but Rob clamped his mouth shut and let Poppa tell him what to do.

It was very hot, but I was still dressed up in my good outfit. We had been to Sunday School and church and had had our big dinner and now had four hours to kill before we'd eat some leftovers— Sunday was the only day that happened—and go back to church for vespers. Schneider Family Tradition called for an afternoon drive in the country. I don't know who enjoyed these excursions. When Rob was away, Poppa drove, Momma sat up front next to him, and neither of us was allowed to speak. When Rob drove, Poppa fussed at him the whole time. I could hardly wait to get home.

We traveled slowly north through the Delaware Valley in a sweaty silence punctuated by Poppa's exhortations. On the way home Poppa suddenly broke all the rules and asked, "How's that girl friend of yours?"

"Peg is just fine," Rob stated in a carefully neutral tone.

From my place in the backseat I could see Rob's eyes in the rearview mirror. He frowned at the road ahead of him.

"I certainly hope you two aren't making any serious plans," Poppa said.

What was going on here, I wondered. We never, ever had conversations like this in our family.

"You're much too young," Poppa continued in the same voice he used to give driving directions, "and so is she."

"Hannah was married when she was twenty," Rob said.

"It isn't just a matter of age."

"Excuse me, I must have misunderstood. I thought you just said it was."

"It's a matter of different backgrounds," Poppa said. "That fellow ahead of you is about to turn left."

"I see that, Father."

"I think Peg is the loveliest little thing," Momma said in a chirpy voice. "A real peach."

"Yes," Rob said, nodding. "Thank you, Momma."

"Look at that, will you? He never even signaled."

"Yes, he did. You just didn't see him."

"I'll never forget her visit at Easter," Momma said. "Just the sweetest person."

I remembered, too: Peg went to church with us, turned out in a smart blue suit with a fox fur-piece draped around her shoulders. When she slipped her dainty kid-gloved hand through the crook of Rob's arm, he glowed with pride at the attention they were attracting.

"What an idiot!" Poppa exclaimed, waving his fist at a car that had dared to pass us.

"She couldn't do enough to help," Momma recalled, faultily. Momma had swathed her in a gigantic apron and let her scrape a few carrots, a safe distance from the sink and stove.

"The plain fact is," Poppa continued, as we moved along at snail's pace with a string of cars building up behind us, "that Peg is too rich for your blood."

"What do you mean by that, Father?" Rob asked in a tight voice with his hands tight on the wheel. Somebody in back of us was honking.

"Her father's a big Pittsburgh lawyer. She dresses like a millionaire's daughter."

"What's wrong with that?"

Two cars shot by us. "Fools!" Poppa yelled. "You'd be better off with Frances Keeler," he said more calmly. "She's more our type of person."

"Frances is a lovely girl," Momma said in her same chirpy voice. "A fine young lady. A peach."

That made two peaches. Poppa was right, though: Frances was as different from Peg as night was from day. Frances was pretty but not beautiful like Peg, and she didn't dress like a fashion model. She and

Rob had gone together all through high school, even though she was a year older. She studied music at a conservatory in Philadelphia, and now she was teaching piano and voice in her mother's parlor.

"Frances and I are friends," he said. "Lifelong friends. But there's no romantic attachment."

I don't know why they stopped going together. Maybe because he met Peg, who would be stiff competition. But on the other hand, I could not imagine Frances ever writing letters like Peg's, telling Rob to be good but not too good and things like that. For some reason Rob had forgotten sweet Frances and was crazy about a girl who made him miserable.

"How come?" I blurted out from the backseat.

Rob's eyes swerved in the mirror, and Poppa hitched around to look at me.

"What did you say?" Rob asked.

"I said 'how come?' How come there's no romantic attachment between you and Frances?"

"Good question," Poppa agreed.

"I don't know, for heavens sake. I left for college. She went her way and I went mine. It happens all the time."

"Sounds to me as though you got some highfalutin ideas up at that school. To let a girl like Frances get away from you for the likes of Miss Baldwin."

Poppa had gone too far. I saw Rob's jaw muscles tighten. Poppa could lecture him on how to handle money and what courses to study in college and what career to have and probably lots of other things, too, but I knew Rob wouldn't like it one bit when Poppa started in on his choice of girl friends, even if Poppa was right.

"Remember how she fed Billy his lunch?" I asked.

Peg had turned back her elegant cuffs and taken the little spoon out of Hannah's hand. "I love babies," she said.

"He's liable to spit it all over you," Hannah warned.

But Peg began to spoon the mush into Billy's mouth, cooing at him and playing peekaboo while she scraped the stuff off his chin and he gurgled and pushed it back at her with his tongue. Rob came into the kitchen to watch.

"Unca Wobbie!" she burbled. "Here's Billy's Unca Wobbie! Dowwwn it all goes for Unca Wobbie! Oh, good Billy, good big boyeee!" And so on and so forth.

"She talked baby talk," I reminded him.

"I don't recall that," Rob said.

" 'Unca Wobbie!' You don't remember how she called you Unca Wobbie?"

"No, I don't."

"I can't imagine how you'd ever marry somebody who talks baby talk," I volunteered. "She might even start talking that way to you."

"Left turn up ahead," Poppa directed. "Start slowing down. Don't forget to signal."

"I doubt it," Rob said, sticking his arm out the

window. "That she'd talk baby talk to me. Peg is very intelligent."

"So's Frances. She's talented, too. She's been around Billy lots of times, and she doesn't talk baby talk to him."

"It would be nice to see Frances," Momma said. "You must invite her to come for dinner soon."

Rob laughed, but there was no laughter in his eyes. "What is this? Is my family ganging up on me?"

"Merely offering a simple observation," Poppa said. "Frances is your type. *Our* type. Peg isn't. Now watch out for that car up ahead. He doesn't seem to know what he's doing."

7

Noticing Otis

I poked a wooden darning egg into the toe of one of my father's socks and slowly stitched a row of black cotton threads across the hole. Next I was supposed to weave the needle back and forth through those threads to make a nice neat darn. But somehow I managed to pull the threads too tight, and the toe puckered into a mean bunch. I yanked out the stitches, and that made the hole larger. The mending basket was full of socks, each worth a penny apiece if competently darned. This was Sock Number One, and any minute now Hannah would come out to check on them.

The week had passed with excruciating slowness. By now Peg had received the compromising photographs and would be writing back to Rob. I had begun to regret the whole thing. It had been a dumb idea to think a couple of snapshots would make a difference. So far there had been no letter, but sooner or later there was going to be. She'd tell him about the pictures, and it would take him approximately eight seconds to figure out who had sent them, probably not much longer to figure out *why*. And then he'd know that I had been snooping in his diary.

What I wanted her to say was, "Dearest Rob, I love you and I'll be true to you always," and not mention the pictures. But what if she wrote something like, "Dear heart, so good to see you disporting yourself with your little chums"? I was going to be in a peck of trouble.

Meanwhile, there was the vow. I didn't look at the diary again, but I studied his face for clues. If he was quiet, did that mean he was unhappy or just tired? When he talked and joked, was he really feeling good or just acting? If the compromising photographs didn't work and Peg wasn't jealous and really didn't care and ditched him anyway, then there was a good chance my brother would end up in Colorado or Wyoming or somewhere. Maybe I ought to attack the problem from a different angle: instead of trying to change Peg's feelings about Rob, I should try to change Rob's feelings about Frances.

I started on a fresh sock, burying Sock Number One at the bottom of the pile. How about a compromising photograph of Frances with somebody? No, that wouldn't do it.

The thing was simply to bring them together again. Well, why couldn't I just invite Frances for dinner? After all, I was her piano pupil, and we were old family friends. Momma liked her. "A peach," she said. She had even said it would be a good idea to ask her to dinner. Grace was her pupil, too. The two of us could invite her over, and I would do all the cooking with Grace as my helper.

Hannah came out, poked her fist into a mended sock, and critically examined my handiwork.

"Hannah, you like Frances, don't you?"

She turned a sock inside out and peered at it. "Oh, yes. Frances is a fine person."

"I thought it would be nice to have her come over for dinner sometime. Since she's my piano teacher and all. And we hardly ever see her anymore."

"That would be nice." The sock passed inspection.

"So if I invited her, if Momma says it's all right, will you help me, Hannah? Because I want her to be my guest and I'll plan the meal and do the cooking and all."

Hannah looked at me with eyebrows arched in surprise. "My goodness," she said. "I'll be glad to help you, Eleanor. Just let me know. But be careful you don't bite off more than you can cook."

I squashed down the lid on the mending basket and went over to Grace's house. Her mother was banging pots and pans around in the kitchen, getting ready to ruin another meal. Compared to Mrs. Bissell, I was a master chef. "Emily Dickinson is upstairs," she said "Go on up."

I rapped on Grace's door.

"Who knocketh?"

"Henry Wadsworth Longfellow," I said. "Robert Browning. Take your choice."

She opened the door a crack. " 'You're my friend— What a thing friendship is, world without end.' That's from 'The Flight of the Duchess.' Browning, of course."

"I didn't know you were memorizing Robert's stuff. I thought you stayed with Elizabeth."

"Well, I do mostly, but he was her true love, and I need to know about him, too, to be sure I can recognize my true love when he comes along. Actually Robert wrote some good things, too, like 'Ah, but a man's reach should exceed his grasp, Or what's a heaven for?' "

"Listen Grace, that's fine, but I have an idea."

"Another one." She sounded bored.

"Yes."

"This one also has something to do with Rob, correct?"

"Correct. But listen, something sensible this time. Nothing crazy. Nothing compromising."

"I can hardly wait to hear about it. Any word from Peg?"

"No. Not yet."

"I think you're going to be in trouble over that one."

"Maybe so. But this new idea will be fine. I think

Rob needs to find somebody new, to make him forget Peg. Not exactly new—actually somebody old, before Peg. I'm thinking of Frances. Rob says they went their separate ways. But I think their ways could be brought together again. And so I'm inviting Frances to come over for dinner, because she's my piano teacher, see, and I'm inviting you, too, and Hannah said she'd help me plan the meal."

"Don't tell me you told Hannah about this?"

"Just that I wanted to have Frances over. Not that I have an ulterior motive."

"Hasn't your family figured out yet that there's an ulterior motive to everything you do?"

"I don't think that's true."

"You're only kidding yourself. Teddie the Schemer, that fits you to a T. So what is it you want me to do this time to aid and abet you? Pose for pictures? Recite poetry?"

"Just moral support, that's all I ask. And maybe help me set the table. I thought we could have a centerpiece, flowers or something, and maybe individual place cards would be nice."

"I'll make them," she said. "That will be fun."

So I asked Momma about it and she said fine. Then I telephoned Frances and invited her to come on Wednesday night and she accepted. Next Hannah and I worked out the menu to make sure I could actually prepare all the things I had listed. We would have pork chops, I decided—two apiece for the men, one each for the women. That made eleven. Better get an even dozen. I would have liked noodles, but Poppa wouldn't eat them, so I'd fix potatoes. I wanted to serve applesauce, but Grace suggested a slice of pineapple on a lettuce leaf with a dab of mayonnaise in the center with half a maraschino cherry, the kind of thing her mother served. I didn't think it sounded good, but it would be colorful and make the table look festive, like a party. I'd make corn muffins and a jelly roll for dessert.

"I can't imagine what's happening to you, Eleanor," Hannah said approvingly. I wasn't used to hearing that tone from her. "I was beginning to think you didn't have a domestic bone in your body. But I see now that you're going to make a wonderful housewife after all, once you settle down to it."

I decided not to argue.

Grace and I ordered the chops from the butcher and got the rest of the groceries. I baked the sponge cake for the jelly roll while Grace worked on the place cards. She drew flowers and vines on little squares of stiff paper with colored pencils. We couldn't decide on names. Should it say "Momma," for instance, or "Mamie," which is what Poppa called her, or "Mary," which was her real name? Grace thought we should use formal titles and printed "Mrs. Schneider" inside a wreath of yellow daisies.

Then we had to decide what the seating plan should be. Should Miss Keeler sit next to Mr. R.

Schneider, or was that being too obvious? We decided to put her directly across the table from him, next to Mr. H. Schneider.

The tricky part about a jelly roll is peeling the paper off the back of the sheet of sponge cake *after* it comes out of the oven *before* you spread on the jelly and roll it up. When I pulled on the paper, the delicate cake ripped, and I was ready to weep.

"Don't worry, Eleanor," Hannah said. "I'll show you how to patch it, and then we'll sift powdered sugar over the top and no one will ever know."

Her sympathy surprised me, and I was grateful.

We had told Momma to rest with her feet up, and we'd take care of everything. Grace and I set the table, put the place cards around, and generally made each other nervous wrecks. She snapped the beans and I peeled the potatoes and browned the chops. The pineapple salads were all arranged. Frances was scheduled to arrive while Rob was taking his bath, so she'd be there as a surprise when he came down.

I was so busy that I hadn't noticed the square white envelope with the back-slanted handwriting on the hall table until it was almost time for Rob to come home, but it didn't take me a split second to decide what to do. I raced upstairs with it and stuck it inside my diary, patted my hair in place, and ran down again.

Rob came in, talking to somebody. A male voice

answered. Rob stuck his head in the kitchen. "Hello all," he said. "I've brought company. This is my partner, Otis."

A shadowy form stepped out from behind my brother and shook hands with Grace and me. The thing I noticed about Otis was his teeth: they were so white, and there seemed to be so many of them. He was not quite as tall as Rob, but he was very good-looking in a movie-star kind of way, even in dirty work clothes.

"Otis is staying for dinner. I hope that's all right. What are you serving tonight?"

"Pork chops," I said, panicking because there would not be enough. I had bought one extra chop, and he would need two. I'd have to give him mine. I decided to tell Rob about Frances. "I've invited a guest, too," I said. "Frances Keeler."

Rob's eyebrows went up. "Really?"

"Your old sweetheart, Rob?" Otis asked, punching Rob's arm.

"She's my piano teacher," I told him.

"We'd better get ready for this," Rob said. "Apparently my little sister is putting on a wingding."

Grace's eyes were as big as dollars. "He's so handsome!" she breathed as they reached the upstairs landing. "He ought to be in movies. Oh, why didn't I put on my good dress? Maybe I have time to go home and change. You've got everything ready now, don't you? I have to make another place card. What's

Otis's last name?"

"Miller." I'd have to fix another pineapple salad,
too.

"Otis can have my pork chop," she whispered on
her way out.

Frances arrived as the mantle clock was chiming
six. I heard the bathtub fill and empty once and fill
again. Momma had come downstairs to learn that
we had an additional guest. With Otis there would
be nine people at the table. Grace returned in her
Sunday dress, smelling of honeysuckle. She had powdered her nose. The potatoes were still hard, but the
beans were turning to mush and the pork chops were
drying out. The corn muffins stuck in the muffin tins
and came out in pieces. Frances had been sent to
the living room to chat with Poppa and Will, who
were bound to notice any minute that dinner was
running late.

We heard two sets of footsteps on the stairs, and
in a flash Grace deserted me. "I don't think it's right
to leave our guest of honor alone, do you?"

"She's not alone, Grace. Momma and Poppa and
Will and Hannah and now Rob and Otis are there.
She has six people to keep her company for ten more
minutes. The potatoes still aren't done."

But we both went into the living room to see what
Rob's reaction would be to Frances. He shook hands
with her and introduced Otis, who had changed into
gray linen plus fours and white silk socks with clocks

embroidered on the ankles. Otis turned on his five-hundred watt smile, took Frances's hand in his and lifted it to his lips. He kissed her hand!

"Charmed, Miss Keeler," he said, looking straight into her eyes, still holding her hand. "Robert has told me a great deal about you."

Frances smiled rosily and two dimples appeared. She pulled her hand away, but not fast enough to satisfy me. I nudged Grace toward the dining room. "We haven't set a place for Otis," I whispered. "Did you bring the place card? I'm going to put him down here next to Momma. Not anywhere *near* Frances."

The potatoes were done, finally, and everything else seemed to be well past done. Momma peeked in, saw that everything was ready, and rang the silver bell. Voices drifted toward the dining room. Frances discovered the place cards, and while everyone found their seats I went out for butter and then rushed in to sit down next to Frances.

Otis was in my seat. The place next to Momma, where I thought Grace had put Otis's card, was the only empty place. Momma held up the flowered card. "It says 'Miss Schneider.' I think this must be you."

"Please stop fussing around and sit down, Teddie," Poppa said, "so we can have the blessing."

I sat down numbly. Otis, who had been talking softly to Frances, holding her chair for her and so forth, turned his toothful smile on me and *winked*. He had switched the cards, of course.

It was Rob's turn, and as usual he sang the doxology. Otis didn't join in with us but simply smiled.

"Don't you like to sing, Otis?" I asked nastily as we started passing the platters.

"Can't carry a tune in a bucket," he said cheerfully, stabbing at a chop.

"Don't think a thing about that," Momma said. "Neither can I. Teddie, I think you've done a lovely job here."

"He may not have a voice, but wait till you hear him tickle the ivories," Rob said enthusiastically, and my heart sank. Something else he had in common with Frances: playing the piano. "Teddie, was this dinner all your idea?"

"Yes," I admitted. "Grace and I wanted to do something in honor of Frances."

"Are you going to make a speech, Teddie?" Poppa asked. He was having a hard time sawing through his chop.

"No," I said. "I haven't even thought of that."

"In that case, I'd like to propose a toast." Toothy Otis stood up and raised his glass of ice water. "To the talented, the beautiful, and the very, very charming Miss Keeler."

We all raised our glasses and took a sip of water.

"Hear, hear!" Rob said.

What a fool, I thought. Otis is going to steal Frances right out from under Rob's nose, and he's not going to do a thing about it.

"Well, I'd like to propose a toast, too," Frances said in a soft, fluty voice. "To Teddie and Grace, who made this lovely meal for us."

Another sip of water. I'm surprised they didn't all choke on it.

You would have thought it was Otis who was the guest of honor, the way the conversation went. He seemed to know something about almost everything —about Poppa's business and the current economic conditions in the country, about Will's church and current trends in religious thinking, about the antics of little Billy, who seemed to be the only one acting normal that evening, and the problems of child-rearing in our society. When he wasn't talking *to* Frances he was talking *for* her. All that wit and charm was for her benefit. And she seemed to be eating it up. What's more, Rob was enjoying it, too— pleased with himself for bringing home such an entertaining friend. Not at all like Warren, who never said boo through an entire meal. Even *Poppa* seemed to be taken in by Otis's easy, graceful manner.

There were chops left over after all. Nobody had gone back for seconds. I served the jelly roll, which had looked fine until I sliced it and the patch job was exposed.

After dinner, when everyone moved toward the living room, Grace and I started glumly to clean up. "Out, you two," Momma said, tying on her apron and flapping us away. "You've worked hard. Go enjoy your company."

Frances was sitting on the piano stool, and someone had brought in a dining room chair so that Otis could sit next to her. She began to play a George Gershwin tune, "Somebody Loves Me," and Otis, at the treble end of the keyboard, improvised a simple embellishment. Then they began doing more complicated stuff. Without saying a word to each other, they moved through some minor harmonics, looking for the key they wanted and the rhythm that suited them. They settled into jazz.

I had never heard piano playing like this, four hands that seemed to be connected to one mind. They went from one tune to another. Usually it was Frances who introduced the next one, and Otis would pick up the melody and fool around with it until he found what he wanted to do, and Frances would follow right along. It was is if they had always played the piano together.

The only one who left was Hannah, taking Billy up to bed. When they stopped nobody could think of anything to say.

"I'll see Miss Keeler home," Otis announced. "Thank you. Thank you all very much."

"Yes, thank you," Frances said, almost in a whisper, hugging me somewhat distractedly.

Otis held the door open for her and they were gone.

"They make a swell couple, don't they?" Will asked.

8

Dancing Lessons

We were halfway through the summer of 1928—
the Roaring Twenties. But the twenties did not roar
at our house. It was the era of Prohibition, when
alcoholic beverages were banned by law. But that
had no effect on the Schneider Family. We never
used them anyhow.

We heard stories about speakeasies and bathtub
gin, though, and Rob even had firsthand experience.
Once he and Otis had run across a man in a flashy
jacket who lounged around a row of trash barrels
near where they were working. Every now and then
a passerby would stop and rummage around in the
trash, come up with an object wrapped in a brown
paper bag, which disappeared immediately into a

pocket, and money would pass into the hands of the dandy.

"A bootlegger," Rob explained to us.

Another time he and Otis needed to get into the basement of a house on South Street to check the telephone lines. The owner, a large woman decked out in a low-cut dress and pounds of jewelry, refused to let them in. She was backed up by three burly men smoking cigars. Rob was ready to give up, but Otis, naturally, talked his way in, assuring them that they were not Federal agents looking for illegal liquor. On their way to the cellar they passed through a dimly lit parlor draped in dusty velvet and littered with empty bottles and overflowing ashtrays.

I loved that scene. "They sound like characters from a Wagnerian opera, didn't they, Poppa?"

Rob laughed. Poppa didn't.

"That will be enough, Son. I don't consider this proper conversation for Teddie's ears or the ears of any other woman, for that matter."

"But—"

That was the end of that. At least he counted me among the women.

We all knew about the Jazz Age, though. I sat on the porch again with the mending, humming Gershwin songs and trying to figure out what I was going to do next about Rob. I had written the Frances dinner off as a fizzle. Otis had taken care of that. According to my calculations. I had two weeks to find somebody for Rob, two more weeks to get them introduced, and two weeks after that for him to fall in love with her (and vice versa) before he was due to leave for school—or for Cheyenne, depending.

I went through my list of prospects. The chief one had just been whisked away by Otis. All of the others were girls from Sunday School. Faye Johnson was awfully skinny, but she dressed well—her shoes and purse always matched. Helen and Lucy Palmer were both very pretty—they had identical marcel waves—but seemed quite stuck on themselves. Sally Clemens was smart and sang well, but she was much too fat. Clara Hebert was cute but dumb. I couldn't think of anyone who was intelligent *and* pretty *and* nice—except Frances. All of the ones I named were crazy about my brother, although the Palmer sisters pretended they weren't interested. When he sang on Sunday mornings with the quartet, they swarmed around him afterwards, telling him what a swell voice he had. The trouble was, he didn't seem to care about any of them. Maybe I needed to come up with somebody entirely different.

I had moved on to shirt buttons when who should come strolling up the walk but Julia, looking cool as a cucumber—quite a change from the last time, when she had been a runny-nosed mess.

"Greetings to the next Amelia Earhart," she said gaily.

Julia checked the seat of the porch chair for dust and sat down, carefully spreading her accordion-pleated skirt and crossing her ankles in the demure fashion favored by mothers.

"You look beautiful," I told her truthfully. "You even look happy."

"I am happy," Julia agreed, smiling serenely. "Life is wonderful."

"It is?"

"Ummm." She gazed at me dreamily. "I want to tell you something. A secret. You're really the only person I can trust. And I'm going to burst if I don't tell somebody."

She made me go through the heart-crossing ritual and then she gave me the astonishing news.

"Tommy and I are getting married!"

"*Married?* But I thought Tommy had been fired and sent away or something and that you'd never see him again!"

"He was, but Teddie—we managed to get in touch with each other—never mind how—and he told me his plans. He left yesterday to go out West and get a job on a ranch. And he's *going* to send for me, and I'm going to go out there to be with him. Isn't that exciting?" She jumped up and twirled around, clapping her hands. Her pleated skirt ballooned around her.

"Where's he going?" I managed to ask. If the trend continued, the West was going to be densely populated with Philadelphians.

"Probably someplace in Montana. Tommy has a cousin around Missoula, and he's going to look him up. Just think of that big blue sky as far as you can see, Teddie, and Tommy and me riding together at sunset. Oh, it's going to be absolutely marvelous!"

I thought of the two of them eating beans out of a can and Tommy spitting into the campfire. "Your mother is going to kill you."

"I know. She wants me to marry a rich business-man or an English nobleman or something, but all I want is to raise horses and babies with Tommy."

"Julia, working on a ranch is not the same as post-ing through Fairmount Park," I pointed out, play-ing my role of wet blanket.

"Of course not; that's not even real riding. *Real* riding is rounding up cattle and things like that."

"You're not old enough to get married, Julia."

"There are places where I am," she said impa-tiently. "We'll go to a justice of the peace, and then later, when things settle down, we'll have a real wed-ding. You could come out and be my maid of honor! For our real wedding I plan to be married very sim-ply, in a little wayside chapel of some sort, with a crown of wild flowers."

I pictured her with daisies and columbine in her hair and said, "I thought Tommy was Catholic. Do they have Catholic wayside chapels? Don't you have to get married in his church?"

She grimaced. "I'm planning to talk him out of that between now and then."

"But how are you going to arrange all this, if he's out in Montana and you're here?"

"I've made a pledge to write every day until we're

together," she said, getting the dreamy look again. "And he's promised to write too, as often as he can. And this is where you come in. Since obviously he can't write to me at home, I'm wondering if you'll be a dear friend and let him write to me here. The letters would come addressed to you. We've agreed that he's not even going to use my name in the letters, just 'dearest' and 'sweetheart,'' so in case they're discovered nobody could trace them to me."

"I don't know, Julia. It sounds awfully risky." It wasn't though; if Momma wondered who I was getting mail from, she wouldn't ask. But then I had an inspiration. "I'll do it, though, Julia, if you'll do something for *me*."

And I told her the story of Rob and Peg and how heartbroken and miserable he was, leaving out the part about the diary but including the part about Otis and Frances.

"I want to find somebody new, to get his mind off Peg. You know lots of people. Can you think of somebody? In your church, maybe?"

"Find him a flapper."

"A flapper?"

"Sure. One of those girls who rolls her stockings below her knees and wears beads dangling down to her waist and lots of makeup and carries a cigarette holder out to *here*."

"How could you suggest somebody like that? Rob wouldn't go for that at all. He likes them sweet and pretty and *nice*."

Julia arched one fine eyebrow and laughed. "That's what *you* think! That's what you *want* to think, what *he* wants you to think, and it may even be what he *thinks* he thinks. But take my word for it, still waters run deep. I'll bet my bottom dollar he's just dying to cut loose with somebody. He doesn't drink, does he?"

"Of course not."

"Well, since you've asked me, I think Rob needs a flapper with a hip flask of bootleg booze, somebody a little bit naughty to take his mind off his broken heart."

"Julia, I thought you'd come up with a couple of sane suggestions. This is crazy."

"Think about it. This could give him a new lease on life."

Julia, who looked as though butter wouldn't melt in her mouth, had the nerve to tell me my brother needed a flapper!

"Wait until you fall in love," she said, standing up and flicking her pleats. "Then you'll find out what the world is really like. Thanks so much for being a friend. You'll let me know as soon as the first letter comes, won't you?" And then she hugged me and danced off the porch.

On the Saturday that was the exact middle of the summer, Poppa went over my weekly accounting of shirts ironed without scorches, edible pies and desserts, wearably mended socks, and other chores, and arrived at a figure of a dollar eighty-eight, to which he generously added a twenty-five cent bonus for the dinner for Frances and for what he called "good effort and attitude." My income was improving, and I kept the money knotted in a sock that even Hannah agreed was beyond mending.

My parents left in a downpour to visit the sick from our church and to get the week's groceries. Hannah and Will had taken Billy to see Will's sister. That left Rob, who was in the living room playing the radio while he pressed his good summer suit. He had actually set up the ironing board in there. I decided it was a good time to teach Grace the proper techniques of making ginger cookies.

Grace was creaming butter and sugar with her bare hands in one mixing bowl, and I was sifting flour and baking soda in another, and we were both humming along with the radio. The music got suddenly louder, and Rob waltzed into the kitchen with an invisible partner.

"May I have this dance?" he asked, bowing to Grace.

She showed him her buttered and sugared fingers. He turned to me. "Madam?"

I dusted my floury hands on my apron. "Yes, but I don't know how to waltz."

"Just follow me." I stumbled before we had gone two steps. "Okay, let me show you a couple of things. Grace, why don't you get that goo off your hands and join us."

We moved into the living room and practiced swaying and counting until we got the hang of it. Rob pushed the ironing board out of the way and put on a phonograph record.

"Ready, Miss Bissell?"

"Flappers don't waltz," she protested, giggling.

"Are you a flapper?"

"Maybe."

"Can you Charleston, then?"

"No."

"All flappers do the Charleston. I'll show you how. Then you can decide if you're a flapper or not."

He changed the record to ragtime. Rob knew all the steps, but we seemed to have two left feet apiece. We bobbed dutifully up and down, trying to follow Rob's rubber-kneed demonstration.

"Now start shifting your weight . . . kick that right heel up and back, but keep your knees close together, like this . . . good! Now move your arms. Get your whole body into it!"

None of us heard the knock at the door. When I glanced up from the cross-knees, which I was finally catching onto, Mr. and Mrs. Bissell were watching us, and they were not smiling. Rob lifted the needle off the record.

"I have never approved of your dancing, Robert," Mr. Bissell said sourly, his jowls wobbling, "or of many of the other things you seem to enjoy, and I do not want you to teach Grace these sinful ways."

"I'm sorry, Mr. Bissell."

"I would suggest that you abandon the Devil's music and find something worthwhile to do with your time. Come along, Grace."

Grace went meekly, tears welling in her eyes. The door shut firmly behind the departing Bissells.

"Oh boy," Rob said. "Where does he get this stuff that dancing is sinful? What a jerk. Poor Grace! Is she really going to be in trouble?"

"Probably. But we may be, too, when the Bissells report on us."

At that moment, with an unbelievable coincidence of timing, Poppa and Momma bumped through the back door, lugging sacks of groceries into the messy kitchen. There was no place to put anything.

"I'll clean it up right away," I said, fumbling with my apron. "It will only take me a minute."

"Teddie, Teddie, Teddie," Momma murmured, surveying the chaos. "It's almost time to start dinner, and there are all these groceries."

"I'll take care of the food, Momma," Rob said. "It's my fault about the mess."

"Your fault? How's that?"

We looked at each other guiltily. "Rob was showing Grace and me some dance steps," I explained, "and we lost track of time."

Poppa looked stern. He didn't think dancing was a sin, but he did consider it frivolous, especially if you were supposed to be doing something else.

During dinner I kept my eyes glued to my plate and was the first to jump up and start clearing when we finished eating, hoping the incident would be quickly forgotten. I was wondering how I could smuggle some cookies over to Grace, when Rob came downstairs looking cool and handsome in his freshly pressed suit, shoes polished, a necktie that I didn't recognize.

"Good night, all," he sang, and on his way out the door he did a couple of Charleston steps and winked at me. Did he have a *date?* Who *with?* He looked much too dressed up to be going somewhere with just Warren.

When the dishes were finished my parents invited me to go a picture show. It was a John Barrymore movie, and they loved Barrymore—"a native Philadelphian," Poppa never failed to mention. Afterward we stopped at the dairy store for a chocolate soda. Apparently I had been forgiven for the mess in the kitchen.

"What an actor!" Poppa raved. "The thing about Barrymore is that wonderful speaking voice. That's because of his training on the stage. I'll never forget his performance of Hamlet a few years ago."

"I'll bet Rob could be just as good as Barrymore," I said, sucking on my soda straw.

"Plenty of movie actors got into trouble when they started making talkies," Poppa continued. "They turned out to have funny, squeaky voices."

"Rob has a good voice," I persisted, ignoring the fact that Poppa had ignored me. "He's a wonderful actor, and he can sing and dance and do all those things. And he's handsome, too. Rob could be a matinee idol. People would rave about Schneider the way they do about Barrymore."

"Aren't you dear to say that about your brother," Momma said.

But Poppa didn't think it was dear. "Actors are all Bohemians, living irresponsible and often dissolute lives. Chances for making a living are very small indeed, unless you happen to be a Barrymore. It's not a life I'd want for any son of mine. Rob is receiving a fine education—or is when he chooses to buckle down and study. A degree in engineering will open many doors for him. Is he entertaining you with such farfetched nonsense?"

"Well . . . not exactly."

"What we don't need in this family is someone with illusions of grandeur. We were put on this earth to toil, Teddie, to work—not to indulge ourselves in idle fancies of fame and fortune."

I slurped at my soda, even though my stomach was starting to ache. I knew that I had no more chance of being the next Amelia Earhart than Rob had of being the next John Barrymore, and it had nothing to do with talent. Rob would be an engineer, I would be a housewife, and if either of us wanted something different, that was too bad.

Momma reached over and squeezed my hand. She didn't know what I was thinking, but she must have known how I was feeling. Dear Momma, always there to soothe and comfort. What if I had had a mother like Mrs. Bissell? When I thought about what it must be like to be in Grace's shoes, I appreciated my own family more—even Poppa, who was now lecturing me on the proper handling of money.

"John D. Rockefeller has always maintained that he saves some, spends some, and gives some away. Are you doing that?"

"Ten percent to the church and the rest in a sock in my drawer."

Poppa nodded approvingly. "Are you saving for a goal?"

"I don't know yet."

But I did know. I wanted a ride in an airplane.

We walked slowly home through damp streets that smelled of honeysuckle (the real thing) and throbbed with the chirr of crickets. The wooden swing creaked on the Bissells' porch. "Hello, neighbors," Mrs. Bissell called out from the darkness. "Come on up and sit a spell."

Momma and Poppa looked at each other. I thought they found the Bissells as hard to put up with as I did.

"Be glad to," Momma said.

"But just for a few minutes," Poppa added. "Tomorrow's the Sabbath and we all need a good night's sleep."

As though anybody needed to be reminded that the next day was Sunday and we had to be at church

before nine o'clock because Poppa was superintendent of the Sunday School as well as teacher of the
Men's Bible Class.

While the adults discussed the relative prosperity
of the tomato plants in their gardens, Grace and I
fidgeted.

"Grace, why don't you take Teddie up to your
room and show her your new shirtwaists," Mrs. Bissell suggested in a syrupy voice.

Glad to escape, I followed Grace's clatter up the
uncarpeted stairs to her bedroom. She closed the door
and faced me with a stricken look.

"I'm not allowed to come to your house for the
rest of the summer."

"Why are they so upset? It was just you and me
and Rob and a phonograph record." I did a cross-
knees, to try to cheer her up.

"Teddie, please don't!" Grace begged. "There's
more. My father is going to use this as a way to get
your father thrown out as superintendent of the Sunday School. He's planning to go before the church
council of elders and tell them about the sinful dancing. He doesn't think anybody who can't bring up
their own children properly should have an influen-
tial position in the church."

Grace burst into tears. I got mad, but before I
could say anything about what a miserable person
her father was, I heard Momma calling up the stairs
that it was time to go home. Poppa had his face shut
tight; I couldn't tell what had happened.

Instead of going straight to bed, I decided to write in my diary. Several days had passed since I had made any entries. When I opened it I found the letter from Peg that I had hidden there the night Frances (and Otis!) came for dinner. I had forgotten all about it.

9

Sheiks and Flappers

A thick, dark cloud of gloom settled over our household. Naturally no one said a word about it. We all pretended that nothing was wrong, that everything was hunky-dory. Nobody mentioned old Bissell or the council of elders. We went to Sunday School and church as though nothing had happened. We ate Sunday dinner as though nothing had happened.

Rob, on the other hand, was in an excellent mood, almost bursting with good cheer. He either didn't notice or decided to ignore the black cloud hanging over Poppa exactly the way, a few weeks ago, Poppa didn't notice or ignored the black cloud suspended over Rob. I wondered where he had gone the night before.

We were eating dessert when there was a knock

at the door. Bissell, I thought. Maybe he's come to apologize.

Rob, apparently expecting someone, jumped up to answer the knock and ushered in three visitors, not Bissell.

First came Marybelle, gawky in an ugly, flowered dress two sizes too big for her, followed by Earl, stuffed into pants and shirt at least one size too small. With them was a girl in a bright green dress with white dots on it as big as silver dollars. The skirt stopped just above her knees, and her stockings were rolled just below them. She had a headband around her wild red curls. A long string of orange beads swung against the belt that rode low on her hips. An ash-tipped cigarette drooped from the ebony holder she held balanced between two fingers.

Rob introduced her. "This is Earl's sister, Beatrice."

"Call me Babe," said the sensational girl in a throaty voice.

Rob went around the table, making introductions. Good manners required Poppa to rise, and he did, stiff as a board. "Miss Potter," he said, but it sounded more like an accusation than a greeting.

Will, who had been stirring sugar into his coffee, stared at her and then he stood up, too. Hannah put on a polite but empty smile. I said, "How do you do?"

Momma said, "We're so pleased to have you here, Beatrice. What a pleasure to meet Earl's sister." Even

Momma sounded a bit hesitant and didn't call her
Babe.

The only one who responded with gusto was Billy,
who cooed and gurgled and waved his chubby arms.

"You're gorgeous!" Babe said in the same throaty
voice, as though she had a cold. "May I pick him
up?"

Hannah said yes, and Babe handed her cigarette
in the extravagant holder to Rob. When she lifted
Billy out of his high chair, he chuckled ecstatically,
clutching at Babe's long string of orange beads. He
gave a delighted yank, the string broke, and beads
flew in every direction, dropping to the floor and
bouncing across the table.

"Oh *damn*," Babe said.

Hannah jumped up, full of apologies, and took
the baby in her arms. Babe laughed a deep, rich
laugh. "It doesn't matter," she said.

Rob and Babe, Earl and Marybelle scooped up
beads, chasing them under the table. I helped. Momma looked sympathetic, Poppa looked displeased,
Will looked condescending, and Hannah looked
worried, as if Billy might get one in his mouth.

"We're going canoeing," Rob explained.

"Babe and I packed a picnic supper," Marybelle
said.

"Don't forget your uke!" Babe reminded Rob.

They left, making a lot of noise. I went to the
front window and watched Earl and Marybelle dis-
appear inside the Essex roadster. Rob and Babe

climbed into the rumble seat, and he put his arm around her shoulders as the car shot away from the curb. It was exactly what Julia had prescribed.

I heard my father say, "This family is headed for perdition."

"Amen," Will said.

Rob must have been very late getting home, because Momma had to call him twice and he appeared at breakfast groggy from lack of sleep. Poppa made some comments about "consideration for others" and "setting a good example"—I guess he meant for me. Rob merely nodded and spooned up his oatmeal. I didn't think the comments had as much to do with staying out late as they did with staying out late with a flapper.

You didn't have to be a mind reader to see that Poppa did not appprove of Babe. "She's from a good family, Henry," Momma said, reminding Poppa that his niece was marrying into it, so it must be all right. Everyone in the family thought well of Marybelle and approved of her choice of Earl. No one had asked me, but I thought he was priggish and dull.

"She's flamboyant," Poppa said.

She wore short skirts and rolled her stockings, she smoked cigarettes in public, and she said "damn." In our family that was more than enough. I hoped Poppa wouldn't try to break it up, because Babe might be the very person who would prevent Rob from running off to the West.

I had remailed the letter from Peg, saw it propped against a vase of flowers when it was delivered for the second time, and watched Rob dash upstairs with it. It had been a completely silly idea, sending those pictures, and I would probably be in a lot of hot water as a result. But my conscience was clear. My only regret was that they hadn't been compromising photographs of Babe, the real thing.

I could hardly breathe, waiting for whatever was going to happen.

But nothing happened. Rob never said a word. His good mood continued. He didn't entertain us with dinnertime stories, saying that most of what he had seen wasn't fit table conversation anyway. That didn't seem to make anybody curious except me. As soon as he finished eating he went out, freshly shaved and nicely pressed.

The Essex stopped often for him. Occasionally the phone rang and a girl's throaty voice asked for Rob. Another square envelope appeared. I struggled daily with the temptation to read Rob's diary *just one more time* to find out what was going on.

Meanwhile Grace was not allowed to come to my house, declared a den of iniquity by her father, and I didn't want to go to her house and run into her stupid parents. The business about the superintendent of the Sunday School would not be settled until the council of elders met at the end of August, an uncomfortable situation since the Bissells' house was separated from ours only by the width of a driveway and a few scraggly azalea bushes.

Grace and I sometimes walked to the schoolyard together to talk, occasionally taking Billy along in his stroller. Grace held him on her lap while we sat on the swings.

"If you could have anything at all that you wanted, when you're grown up," Grace asked, "what would it be?"

My ready answer: "A farmhouse with a smooth, grassy field with a windsock at one end and a barn with a yellow airplane at the other."

"I can't believe that you don't want a husband and children. It's not *normal* to want to live by yourself. I think it even says something about that in the Bible."

I hated it when Grace tried to prove I was wrong by quoting from the Bible, a trait inherited from her father. But before that could develop into a full-blown argument, Julia appeared outside the school-yard wall, a large straw hat squashed down over her hair. Her mood this time was subdued.

"I was on my way over to your house, Teddie," she said, glancing at Grace.

There had been no letter from Tommy addressed to me. I shook my head to let her know that, and she pressed her lips together to keep them from trembling. I chattered about Billy until she seemed composed again. Billy babbled and grinned, displaying eight perfect white teeth.

"I think we'd better be getting home," I said after a while.

The sidewalk was too narrow for the three of us, so Grace went on ahead with Billy in the stroller. "No letter?" Julia whispered.

"Nothing."

We walked on in silence. "May I have a glass of water, Teddie? I'm so thirsty I could die." Grace looked unhapppy about not being able to come in with Julia and me.

"I'll see you later, Grace," I promised. "There's a ball game tonight, don't forget."

"He's been gone for seventeen days," Julia hissed as soon as Grace was out of earshot, "and not a word in all that time! How long do you think it would take him to get to Montana?"

"How was he going to get there?"

"Taking a train as far as he could. Then he didn't know. He doesn't have much money. Oh, I don't know what to think! I was sure I'd hear from him by now!"

"I guess you can't write to him, either."

"I've been writing him in care of General Delivery in Missoula. He promised to send me his address as soon as he got settled." She was tying knots in her linen handkerchief.

"Well, then, that must be it, Julia," I said in what I hoped was a comforting way. "He isn't settled yet."

Then I had an inspiration. "Maybe he already has a job as a cowboy, and he's riding the range hundreds of miles from the nearest post office. Cheer up, Julia," I told her. "You know that he misses you just as much as you miss him. He probably falls asleep by the campfire every night thinking of you."

Julia smiled. "I know. But when you're in love, life isn't complete without your loved one. In fact, it's just plain misery."

We took glasses of ice water out on the porch, after I had delivered Billy to Hannah. I tried to find things to talk about, but Julia was stuck on one subject, like a broken record. I tried to convince her to go to the ball game with Grace and me, but she wasn't interested in anything that wasn't connected with Tommy.

"You'll let me know just as soon as a letter comes, won't you?"

I promised I would. Julia left, and I made up my mind that if this was what love was all about, I would never have any part of it.

Grace and I sat on the top row of bleachers and watched my brother's softball team go down to ignominious defeat at the hands of First Methodist. Quite a few people turned out to cheer for their Sunday School teams, and the main reason Grace and I were there was to see who else would show up. We spotted Warren Jennings wandering around with his camera, waiting for a good action shot. He must have had a long wait, because it was an unusually tedious game.

We watched Rob strike out once, pop a fly that fell into the fielder's glove as though guided by fate, get tagged coming into third. Out in the field he fumbled several fairly easy catches. Either he seemed to be nowhere near the ball or—worse—it seemed to drop straight through his glove.

"He should stick to dancing," Grace said.

"It's just an off night," I said defensively, even though I thought she was right.

The Methodists were up. They were good hitters. Run after run was batted in. The score was embarrassingly lopsided.

"Julia used to come to these games," Grace said.

"Yes." She was always surrounded by a reverent cluster of boys, too, I remembered.

"Something's *wrong* there."

"I wouldn't say that anything's wrong exactly," I said, wondering if it might be all right to tell Grace about the letters that weren't coming. I decided not to. "She just misses Tommy."

"It's more than that. I just have a feeling."

Grace was always having "feelings," and the thing of it was that she often turned out to be right. I was afraid she might be right about Julia.

As we were walking home from the ball field, Grace asked, "When is Hannah's baby coming?"

"I don't know what you're talking about. *What* baby?"

"Hasn't she told you yet? Hannah's going to have another baby."

I shook my head, hurt that Grace knew something about my family that I didn't know. "No. Did she tell *you*," I asked, feeling mean, "or just your mother?"

"Didn't have to. You can tell by looking at her. Her face is softer. There's a look in her eyes. Haven't you noticed that?"

I hadn't.

Warren and Rob chugged by in Warren's old Ford, put on the brakes, and backed up. "You lovely ladies like a ride home?"

I would have accepted—my shoe was rubbing a blister on my heel—but Grace squeezed my arm hard. "No, thanks. We'd rather walk," she called out, and the Ford puttered off. "If I'm not allowed to come your house, I can imagine the trouble I'd be in if I got in the same *car* with Rob."

"I'm sorry, Grace. I forgot."

We walked on in silence, inhaling whiffs of honeysuckle.

"Warren Jennings is in love with you, you know."

Just like that. Out of the blue. In a tone of absolute sureness.

"No, I do not know any such thing. Grace Bissell," I sputtered, "that is the dumbest thing, the *craziest* thing, I have ever heard in my life. Have you taken leave of your senses?"

"No," Grace said calmly. "I'm not dumb, and I'm not crazy. I'm intuitive, remember? Intuitive types pay closer attention than logical types."

"Like me?"

"Like you. You're logical, and you miss things. What I say is true: Julia is in trouble, Hannah is in a family way, and Warren Jennings is in love. With you."

How can you argue logically with someone's intuition? I kept mumbling that she was out of her mind, et cetera, but I thought I'd better make some notes about this in my diary.

Poppa always took his vacation the second week of August, and we always went to the same place, Ocean City, New Jersey, and stayed at the same hotel, Seagull Manor, a four-story wooden firetrap a few blocks back from the boardwalk. We always took the train to the shore because Poppa hated to drive long distances, but this year there was to be a change. Rob would drive us down and stay overnight with his friends at the ritzy hotel where he'd worked as a waiter the summer before. Then he'd take the car home and come back for us the next weekend.

We only stayed a week, but it took us at least two weeks to get ready, hauling the folding chairs and beach towels and such down out of the trunk in the attic, going over our wardrobes. Momma decided that I needed a new bathing suit. I wanted a form-fitting woolen one, but Momma didn't think that style was appropriate and so she made me a sort of dress with bloomers under it, very sweet and old-fashioned. I hated it.

The evening before we left, Warren came over and helped Rob work on the car, tuning it up for the trip. Of course he stayed for dinner, demolishing most of a large pot roast. Warren must have eaten hundreds of meals at our house, and this was the first time I had ever been uncomfortable with him there. A member of the family, practically, had become a stranger, worse than a stranger, and it was all Grace's fault. At least I didn't have to sit next to him. He was at the other end of the table.

"Warren, why don't you ride along down to the shore with us tomorrow?" Rob suggested when seconds were being passed around. "I'm sure I could get you a place to bunk."

"What a grand idea," Momma said. "Then Rob won't have to make the trip home by himself."

Poppa agreed. He thought Warren had more sense than Rob about driving, but he didn't come right out and say that.

"Is there enough room in the car?" Warren asked.

Everyone thought there was, although it was clear to me that there wasn't.

I was carrying in dishes of blueberry cobbler, divided up to serve seven instead of six, when Will cleared his throat and began to speak in his preacherly way.

"Hannah and I have something we are especially thankful for, and we want to tell you our good news before you leave." Dramatic pause to make sure he had our attention, and then he continued, "Hannah is with child." Hannah kept her eyes modestly lowered during Will's announcement.

Momma smiled happily, and I guessed she already knew. She got up and hugged my sister.

"Well, well, well," Poppa said. "And when is the blessed event?"

"February," Will said.

"Congratulations," Rob said, and Warren echoed him. They both went around the table to shake Will's hand and to kiss Hannah.

"I hope it's a girl, don't you?" I said. Hannah nodded but Will said, "Whatever the Lord sees fit to bless us with."

After supper I broke down and went over to Grace's to say good-bye. We wouldn't see each other for two weeks, because the day before we were to come back she was leaving with her parents for their week's vacation in the Poconos. They stayed in a rustic cabin with no electricity and a wood stove for cooking. Grace and her mother hated it, but old Bissell liked to rough it.

"You were right about Hannah," I said.

"Of course."

"I sure hope you aren't right about Warren. He's driving down with us."

Grace thought that was the funniest thing she had heard in days. "Don't do anything I wouldn't do," she said with a cackle. I could have killed her.

Warren showed up the next day in time for lunch. Then Rob fitted Warren's overnight bag in the trunk with the rest of the luggage and they debated who was going to sit where. They decided what I already knew: he'd be crammed in the back seat with me in the middle between him and Momma, all six feet and a couple of inches of him. He flattened himself against the door, and I leaned toward Momma, and that's how we made the journey.

It was a relief to arrive at Seagull Manor and have our bags carried upstairs and see Rob and Warren go off together. But before they left, Poppa, now getting into the vacation spirit, suggested that we all have Sunday dinner together after church the next day.

We had a large room on the top floor with a double bed and a cot; we also had the only private bath on the floor, a luxury that Poppa insisted upon. I hurried into the bathroom to put on my new bathing suit. It made me look like a ruffled barrel.

"Doesn't she look sweet, Henry?" Momma asked.

"Indeed she does," said Poppa, ready to doze off for the first nap of his vacation. The trip had worn him out, navigating for Rob.

Momma and I went to the beach without him. Momma had her knitting, a sweater for Rob in his school colors, and soon she was settled on her wicker beach chair. The tide was out, and I decided to go for a walk—north, away from the big hotels and any possibility of running into Rob and Warren. This might be the summer for long, solitary walks, I thought.

The next day we met at the big church near the boardwalk, and we all sat together, me at one end of the pew and Warren at the other. Then we walked back to Seagull Manor; Momma and I brought up the rear.

Meals were served in a dining room paneled with dark wood and decorated with dingy brown wallpaper. Mrs. Cassidy, the fat, grouchy woman who was the owner and cook, slapped the food down in front of us almost as a dare, except for Poppa, whom she fussed over. I thought of claiming a stomachache so I wouldn't have to sit through another meal with Warren, but I was hungry. Mrs. Cassidy, who did not believe in seconds, nevertheless brought an extra serving of dessert for Poppa, who passed it on to Warren.

"You're a much better cook than Mrs. Cassidy," Warren whispered across the table to me.

"That's not saying much," I whispered back, but even that bit of conversation made me so nervous that I really did end up with a stomachache.

It had begun to rain while we were eating. Rob and Warren decided to go for a walk on the boardwalk in spite of the weather. Poppa settled down with the Sunday paper. Momma knitted. I viewed sepia-toned scenes of ancient Greece and Rome through a stereoscope. The lounge at Seagull Manor was almost as gloomy as the dining room, and I had seen all the stereoscope scenes many times before. Rob and Warren came back to pick up the car and to listen to Poppa's lecture on the best route to take, safe driving practices, and so on, a lecture as familiar as the pictures of the Parthenon and the Colosseum. I was relieved when they left and my stomach gradually returned to normal.

It rained every day that week but one. Momma knitted contentedly in the lounge. The bad weather didn't bother her at all, but Poppa took it as a personal affront. This was his only week of vacation, the only chance he'd have to play miniature golf, his favorite sport.

On Friday, the rain stopped, but the skies remained overcast. I went to the beach anyway, sick and tired of stuffy rooms full of mildewed furniture. I had my diary with me, but there was nothing to write except that I was bored and wanted to go home —even though I dreaded the trip back squashed between Momma and that person who made me so nervous.

10

Babe

On Saturday the clouds lifted, and we were on the beach by nine o'clock. Every so often Poppa stretched and strolled down to the water and stood there up to his knees, arms folded above his stomach, staring out to sea. Momma padded along looking for shells. When she saw one she liked, she stooped down, knees wide apart, to pick it up.

I hated the sight of my parents in bathing suits: Poppa with his sloping stomach and skinny legs and white skin; Momma with knots of purple veins on her chubby calves. She took the corn plasters off her little toes so the salt water could soothe them. They seemed not to know or care how bad they looked. When they weren't splashing around in the shallow water, they sat in beach chairs under a striped umbrella.

At noon we bought hot dogs and soda pop from a vendor, even though Momma was afraid the meat might not be good. I waited an hour and then went back into the water. I wasn't a good swimmer. My method was to dash in until a wave came along and chased me. Sometimes it caught up, tumbling me under its lip and dragging me over the rough bottom. That scared me, but I went back for more.

When I finally came out, exhausted, Poppa said we should get ready to go back to the hotel to pack and get cleaned up. Rob would be arriving soon, and we could all go out for a nice dinner, a special treat on our last night at the shore.

"Where shall we go?" Momma asked.

"Atlantic City," I said.

"Too much honky-tonk," Poppa said. "There's a seafood house on the bay that's cheap enough to feed Warren."

I had managed to forget about Warren.

Momma was winding up her yarn when I saw Rob making his way toward us over the hot sand. The person with him was not Warren but Babe, wearing a kind of Chinese robe of brilliant colors and bold oriental designs. She wore sandals that showed off the bright red nail polish on her toes. A large paper parasol was propped against one shoulder, and her cigarette holder swung in her free hand.

"I brought along a surprise," Rob said, grinning.

"Hello hello!" Babe called cheerfully, and of all things she gave my *father* a hug. Not my mother, which might have been acceptable; my *father*. She dropped her parasol on the sand, flung her arms around his neck, planted a loud kiss on his cheek, and said, "Mr. Schneider, you big huggy-bear, you!"

Momma said, "My, my."

Rob said, "We thought we'd surprise you."

Poppa said, "You certainly have."

I was relieved and pleased because it wasn't Warren.

Rob spread out two beach towels, and Babe dropped her Chinese coat next to the parasol, revealing a formfitting black bathing suit that showed off every curve. She pulled a white bathing cap over her red curls and seized Rob's hand.

"Come on, sweetie," she said. "Time for a swim!" She ran toward the water, towing Rob after her.

"My stars," Momma said.

"That is an impudent young woman," Poppa said. "Impudent as well as flamboyant. I believe Robert has taken leave of his senses."

Rob and Babe jumped over a few low waves and dived in. It was plain soon enough that Babe easily outdistanced Rob, swimming far out beyond the other bathers until a lifeguard shrilly whistled her back.

They ran up on the sand together, arms around each other. When Peg had visited, she had merely tucked her hand in the crook of his arm, or he took her elbow to assist her. Babe clearly didn't need help with anything, but Rob couldn't seem to keep his hands off her. And vice versa.

"Did you see this gal swim? She's a real athlete, a lot better than I am."

"Honey, it just takes a little practice," Babe said.

First sweetie, now honey. We did not use pet names in our family. Babe didn't know that yet.

Poppa rolled his newspaper into a tight cylinder and whacked the arm of his chair with it. "We're going back to get ready for dinner," he said stiffly. "Would you and Miss Potter care to join us, Son?"

It was the kind of invitation Rob was supposed to refuse, but he either ignored Poppa's tone or wasn't listening. "You bet. We're going to stretch out here in the sun for a while, and then we'll meet you at the Gull. About six?"

"Five-forty-five," Poppa corrected.

Babe chirped, "See you later!" and fitted a cigarette into her holder.

Poppa marched off with our beach umbrella under his arm like a sword. Momma and I scrambled to collect our things and catch up with him.

"I can't think where he found that . . . that flapper," Poppa huffed as we climbed the third flight of stairs to our room. "She is extremely brash and very unladylike."

"She's Earl's sister, Henry," Momma reminded him again. "It isn't as though he just *found* her somewhere. Marybelle introduced them."

"I don't care whose sister she is," Poppa declared. "She's not the kind of young woman I expect our son to be attracted to."

We took turns using the bathroom, and it was a slow process for all of us to get bathed and dressed. Momma began packing our bags while we waited for Poppa to finish.

"Look at yourself, Teddie," Momma said, pointing me toward the mirror. "You're sunburned."

My shoulders were bright red and starting to hurt.

We were sitting on the green rocking chairs lined up on the broad front porch when our Chevy pulled up. The doors sprang open, and Rob jumped out one side and Babe out the other, without waiting for him to come around to help her. She had on a yellow sleeveless dress with a deep V that showed off her tanned and freckled skin. She smiled and waved and ran up the steps ahead of Rob, who followed with the same silly grin he had been wearing since they arrived. Poppa started to rise as he always did when a lady approached, but he sat down again, glaring.

"My, don't you look sharp!" Babe said to Poppa. "A real sheik!"

He didn't look like a sheik at all. He looked like a paunchy man in a seersucker suit. Babe bent over and kissed him on his bald spot, apparently not detecting the coolness that made our end of the porch feel like an icebox.

But Rob must have noticed it, or at least seen Poppa's jaw drop. "Mail call!" he said too heartily, producing a sheaf of envelopes from his pocket, the week's accumulation. There were four letters for Momma, the family correspondent who kept in touch with relatives on both sides of the family. And there was one addressed to me.

" 'Miss Eleanor Schneider,' it says here," Rob announced, examining the envelope. "The postmark is Missoula, Montana. I didn't know you knew anyone in Montana."

"I don't really," I said.

"Well, apparently somebody there knows *you*." He handed me the letter.

There was no return address. I folded it in half and slid it into my pocket.

"Aren't you going to open it?"

"Later."

"Aren't you curious?"

"It can wait."

This now had everyone's attention. Then Babe said, "I'll bet Teddie has a beau! Anybody as cute as Teddie probably has dozens of boyfriends, and why not in Missoula, Montana? Why, I'll bet it's a cowboy!"

This made matters much worse. I could not think of a thing to say.

Babe put her arm around my scorched shoulders. "I didn't mean to embarrass you, but you are just as cute as the dickens." She let go of me and linked her arm through Rob's. "It's private," she said, "and a woman is entitled to her privacy."

I didn't know how I felt about Babe at that moment—whether to thank her or to start to bawl.

Rob said, "Righto! There's nothing like a big secret! Now folks, where are we going to dine this evening?"

Poppa's lips were a tight, straight line. "The Clam Box," he said shortly.

Without any hesitation Babe climbed into the front seat next to Rob, where Poppa always sat. *Always*. But he helped Momma into the back seat, waiting until I crawled in the middle, and crowded in after us.

Babe turned halfway around in her seat and made conversation, mostly by asking questions: how the weather had been, what we had done all week, what the food was like at Seagull Manor. Momma gave all the answers.

When he had found a suitable table and ordered our meal, Poppa asked, "Are you a student, Miss Potter, or are you employed?"

"I'll be a junior at Sarah Lawrence," she said. "I'm studying history, and I'm planning to be a journalist."

"A journalist? What kind of journalist?"

"A newspaper reporter," she said. "My main interest is politics. Someday I'm going to be the Washington correspondent for *The Philadelphia Inquirer*."

Now Babe had Poppa's attention. He loved to discuss politics. He and Will argued all the time, even though they were both Republicans. How did she think the presidential campaign was going, he wanted to know.

"Just dandy," Babe said. "I think Smith has a good chance of taking it."

"*Smith?* My dear young lady, I can't believe I heard you correctly."

The debate raged on through dinner. It amused Babe, who was a Democrat, and infuriated Poppa, who found it inconceivable that anyone could favor Alfred E. Smith, a Roman Catholic and a Democrat backed by Franklin D. Roosevelt, whom my father viewed as the archenemy of society. Poppa's opinion was that only the lower classes would vote for Smith.

"What about your brother?" Poppa roared, while Momma tried to shush him. Other diners were looking at us. "Is he a Democrat, too?"

Babe laughed in her throaty way. "Yes, but Earl doesn't give a hoot about politics," she said. "All he cares about is making money. He plays the stockmarket. I think he dreams about the ticker tape at night."

Poppa looked relieved. "Earl is a sensible fellow," he said, more quietly.

"I think your father is absolutely adorable," Babe said to Rob. "It's not often I find a man who wants to discuss serious subjects and really gets his heart into it."

"I didn't know you were so serious, Babe," Rob

said, not entirely pleased.

"Don't judge a book by its cover, honeybun," she said and turned her attention to her steamed clams.

You can't imagine the shock waves that rolled through our family when Rob and Babe did not appear at the Sunday morning church service. Momma and I were sent ahead to save five seats, while Poppa hovered near the entrance until the opening hymn. He finally left word with the usher where we could be found, but the service ended and there was still no Babe and no Rob.

"I told them last night we were leaving right after lunch," Poppa fumed.

"I hope nothing's happened," Momma fretted.

They were sitting in the car in front of Seagull Manor. Rob had his arm around Babe, and they were deep in conversation. They hardly noticed us until we were standing next to the car.

We ate our last meal in the Gull's dining room. Babe ignored Poppa's chilly silence and explained why they hadn't been in church. They had gone to an Episcopal service in Atlantic City.

"That's a service I've never much cared for," Poppa said disapprovingly. "Might as well be Catholic."

Babe smiled. "It takes getting used to," she said.

"Is your family Episcopalian?" Momma asked.

"Oh, yes. There's even a bishop in there somewhere."

"And Earl?"

"Sure. But Marybelle is insisting that he leave and join her church. She's a swell girl, but she can be very stubborn. She won't even come to St. Stephen's and see what it's like."

"It's a beautiful service, Father," Rob said. "The priest wears embroidered robes. The music is wonderful. It's almost like watching an opera. You'd like it on aesthetic grounds if nothing else."

"I doubt it," Poppa said stubbornly. "I prefer to worship God in simplicity."

"I couldn't agree with you more, Mr. Schneider," Babe said—unexpectedly, I thought—and changed the subject to me and what I would be studying in school. I didn't like being the center of attention, but it was better than another argument.

We were driving west across southern New Jersey toward Philadelphia, Babe in the back seat with Momma and me, which turned out to be the second smart thing she had done that day. Poppa directed Rob's driving as usual. After about a half hour of "Slow down" and "Watch out," Babe made a suggestion: "Let's all sing!"

She started "In the Evening by the Moonlight" in a fine, rich alto, and Rob joined in immediately on the harmony. I half expected Poppa to say this would interfere with Rob's concentration on the road or was improper for the Sabbath, but he didn't. Then Babe went on with "Down by the Old Mill Stream" and "On Moonlight Bay" and some other old favorites. We sang all the way home. Poppa was actually smiling by the time we pulled in front of the house. Babe had figured out the surest way to charm him.

Hannah came out to meet us with the news that Billy had taken his first steps. Momma invited Babe to stay for supper. She held Billy on her lap and didn't seem to mind when he drooled on her dress. It was a pleasant meal. Neither politics nor religion came up. Poppa even said we'd skip vespers this once. Everything was fine, except my sunburn.

I wondered if Rob was in love with Babe. He looked happier than he had all summer. I wondered if he would want to marry her and what Poppa would say. She'd never put up with living in the same house with all the rest of us; she was much too independent. Even if they came just for Sunday dinners and holiday picnics, it would be nice, though. Maybe someday I could talk to Babe about my wanting to be an aviatrix. She was going to be a career woman; she'd understand. Maybe she'd have some advice about convincing Momma and Poppa—especially Poppa—that my ambition was a good thing.

Rob was getting ready to drive Babe home when Poppa said, "Son, I need to discuss an important matter with you—*if* you happen to get in at a decent hour." You couldn't miss that tone.

"I'll be back in two shakes of a lamb's tail," Rob said. "I have to hit the hay early. The boss is leaving on vacation tomorrow, and I'm supposed to be at work by seven."

I went up to my room and tried to get interested in *Gulliver's Travels*. I wished Grace were home. I needed somebody to talk to. After a while I heard the car in the driveway, the door slam, Rob's and Poppa's voices on the stairs, Rob's bedroom door close. Silence.

I had the awful feeling that the "important matter" to be discussed was Babe. Poppa could see how much Rob liked her but couldn't stomach the idea of an impudent, flamboyant, Episcopalian, Democratic career woman, and he was going to put the kibosh on the whole thing. I would have bet every nickel in my sock that's what was happening in the next room—and I would have given a lot of those nickels to know. Eavesdropping didn't work; I tried but I couldn't hear a thing.

After a while the door opened and voices said good night. One by one the rest of the family came upstairs and went to bed. The house was very quiet. Inside me a small lump of anger was beginning to swell like dough. That and the sunburn kept me awake for a long time.

Momma's crochet hook darted speedily around an antimacassar she was making for Marybelle's engagement shower, planned for Labor Day.

"I'm going over to Julia's for a little while," I said.

"Such a lovely girl. How is she? I haven't seen her in an age." I wondered if Momma remembered Mrs. Bissell's juicy bit of gossip.

"Just fine," I said, thinking she really would be when I gave her Tommy's letter.

"Say hello to her dear mother for me."

"I will, if she's home." I hoped she wouldn't be.

But Mrs. Gibbs answered the bell and invited me in.

"Julia's not here," she said. "Sit down, Teddie. Can I get you anything? You'll have to excuse me, I'm not feeling too well." She didn't look well either, as though she had been crying a lot but had run out of tears.

"Where's Julia?"

"She's gone to Alabama. We found a lovely school there for young ladies that's far better than anything around here." Mrs. Gibbs tried a smile but it didn't work. I couldn't believe what I was hearing. "Julia went down early to get adjusted before classes begin. She'll spend the year there and come home next summer." All of this came out in disjointed sentences.

Julia hadn't said a word to me about any school in Alabama, and I could not imagine that she had left so abruptly, without even coming over to say good-bye.

"Can you give me her address? I want to write to her." I could send Tommy's letter, too, I thought. Now he'd be able to write to her directly.

Mrs. Gibbs pressed her fingers against her forehead, making a cage over her eyes. "I'm sure she'd like to hear from you, Teddie. But I must warn you that it's a very strict school and all of the girls' mail is screened. The housemother reads whatever she gets and whatever she sends." Mrs. Gibbs shuffled through the drawer of a rickety desk, apparently searching for a pencil and paper that were lying in plain sight. "In the south," she continued, locating the paper and writing out the address, "young ladies are much more strictly supervised than they are here. Unfortunately, my Julia has done some . . . foolish things." Her voice cracked and she began to sob, a dry sound like a cough.

I patted her on the shoulder. Nobody cried like this at my house, but nothing really awful had happened there. *Yet.* "I'll write to her," I said and rushed down the stairs and away from that sad place. My problem wasn't solved, and now I had a new one to worry about.

There seemed to be no way to get Tommy's letter to Julia if somebody was reading her mail. Alabama was a long distance to send a girl just to break off a romance her mother didn't approve of, especially when her sweetheart was thousands of miles in another direction.

I decided to write Julia a letter with a secret message spelled out in code, to let her know that he had written. Then I would send Tommy's letter back to him with a note telling him what Mrs. Gibbs had

said, giving him Julia's address, and warning him
that all her mail was being read by the housemother.
I'd explain our secret code. After that it was up to
him. True love would find a way.

In order to get Tommy's address so I could do all
of this, I would have to open his letter, just like the
Alabama housemother. I said a prayer explaining to
God that this was necessary, not at all the same as
snooping, and slit open the envelope.

The return address was not at the beginning of
the letter, where we had been taught to put it, but
printed at the end. It was impossible not to see the
few lines above it: "I don't know what to say about
the baby. There isn't any way I can help you, as I
have not found steady work and am doing odd jobs
here for my cousin. Marriage is out of the question.
It would be best for you to forget about me. Take
care of yourself, that's the important thing. Good
luck, Tommy."

I folded the letter and slipped it back in the envelope.

Poor Julia.

Now I understood that she was not going to a
fancy finishing school after all. That was her mother's pathetic story. And poor Mrs. Gibbs! It did
seem that Julia's life was ruined. Now she would
never be able to marry a nobleman or a wealthy
businessman or whatever it was her mother had in
mind for her. How could she have gotten herself

into such a mess?

I had heard rumors about this sort of thing. An older girl from our church had once disappeared for a few months, and her parents told everyone she had gone to help an aunt who was sick. But Momma decided to tell me the truth: "It does sometimes happen that girls who aren't married have babies. It's a tragic thing for everybody when that happens. Good people save themselves for marriage."

Julia had not saved herself.

And the worst of it was, Tommy didn't even love her. He didn't want to marry her after all, even though she had sacrificed her virtue. If he did, he wouldn't have written that kind of letter. Mr. Slawson at the stables had probably been right about him.

I wondered how it felt to be in Julia's shoes. Guilty, probably, and lonely and scared. And when she found out that Tommy wasn't going to marry her, she'd be brokenhearted, too. Mrs. Bissell would say she deserved it, that God was punishing her for her sin.

I wrote to Julia in the code she and Grace and I used in grammar school, hoping she'd remember it and no one else would catch on:

"Dear Julia,

Excitement and such joy you must feel! Up here in New Zealand I put on size 6 boots each Sunday evening and hike to our peaceful Sunday fellowship. Yesterday 223 neighbors left our town until January tenth. I plan to visit my brother soon."

If she copied down the underlined letters, she'd get this: XSJUFUPNNZDPSZBOTESVHTUPSF223NBSLFUTUNJTTPVMB. And if she moved each letter *backward* in the alphabet, so that all the B's became A's and so on, and moved the numbers backward, too, fitting in the spaces, the message would read: WRITE TOMMY C O RYANS DRUGSTORE 112 MARKET ST MISSOULA.

Heaven knew whether that would make it past the housemother's eagle eye. It did sound pretty strange. Grace was a whiz at this code. She could write a perfectly normal-looking sentence with an elaborate message buried inside. I was a rank amateur by comparison.

Then I described my week in Ocean City, except for the part about Warren. I wanted to tell her all about Babe and Rob and Poppa, but I wasn't sure if that was censorable or not, and I didn't have the patience to put the whole story in code. I wanted to tell her about Hannah "being with child," as Will put it, but I was afraid that might make her feel bad. I wondered what would happen to Julia's baby; probaby they would give it away to people who wanted it. Surely it wouldn't have to grow up in an orphanage or anything like that. Imagine having a baby and then giving it away. It must be awful.

"I miss you a whole lot," I wrote. "I hope you're

meeting lots of nice girls and having a good time."
I wished I could say what I was really feeling. But
I wasn't even supposed to *know*.

Next I wrote to Tommy, telling him what I
thought of his faithlessness, and then I tore up that
letter and wrote another one, giving him her address
and a short explanation of the code. Then I thought
of her getting a letter from him with "There isn't
any way I can help you" buried in it, and I tore that
one up, too. Let her believe he still loved her for as
long as she could.

11

Carried Away

When it was almost time for Rob to come home, I took Julia's letter to the mailbox on the corner and hung around until I spotted him striding along from the depot.

"Fancy meeting you here," he said, with the smile that I now recognized as meaning he didn't feel as good as he wanted you to think.

"Hi! How was your day?" My hearty tone was just as phony as his smile.

"Fair to middlin'. How about yours?"

"Okay," I fudged, true to Schneider Family Tradition. I couldn't tell him about Julia, and I couldn't ask him what was wrong. "What happened today?"

"The boss went on vacation and left us swamped with work, Otis had a heavy date last night and wasn't worth a plugged nickel all day, it was ninety-two degrees in the shade, and I feel as if I've been run over by a steamroller."

I wondered if Otis's heavy date was with Frances, but of course I didn't ask. We walked the rest of the way home in silence.

It was Rob's turn to ask the blessing. He didn't sing it this time; he *said* it, rattling through a mile a minute to get it over with. Hannah glanced at him curiously but said nothing.

"Well," Momma said cheerfully, "it surely was a nice vacation, wasn't it, Teddie? We had a wonderful time, didn't we, Henry? And I'm sure Hannah and Will had a good time without all of us underfoot."

Yes, Hannah said; they had had a nice time, too. They hadn't done as much as they had planned, though, because Billy came down with a fever and Hannah hadn't been feeling too well herself. No, nothing serious for either of them.

When the meat platter was passed around a second time, Will decided not to take the extra lamb chop, since he seemed to be putting on weight. He offered it to Poppa. Poppa refused the chop and offered it to Rob. Rob accepted it. The only time they spoke to each other was to talk about that chop.

Anybody could see that something was out of kilter, but nobody said a word. We dabbed mint jelly on our lamb chops and saved room for the rice pudding as though everything was just peachy. It was clear to me that Poppa was the cause of whatever was wrong.

As I saw it, there were several things Rob could do.

One: Defy Poppa openly and keep going out with Babe, no matter what. It was Rob's life and he could do what he pleased, including falling in love with a flapper. But it wasn't Rob's *money*. Poppa was paying for Rob's education, and he'd probably stop if Rob didn't do what Poppa wanted. Still, if Rob really loved her, he'd work his way through school.

Two: Defy Poppa secretly. But Julia had defied her mother secretly, and look where it got her. Rob wasn't the type to defy Poppa either secretly *or* openly. (Neither was I.)

Three: Accept Poppa's edict, stop seeing Babe, and put on a stiff upper lip and a false smile—a neat trick that the Schneider family had worked out perfectly.

Four: Go out West and get a fresh start. That's what I'd do if I were Rob.

On Thursday evening Poppa dressed in the suit usually reserved for Sundays and drove alone to the church to meet with the council of elders on old Bissell's censure motion charging that Poppa's son didn't behave like a Christian gentleman and therefore Poppa should not serve as superintendent of the Sunday School. Illogical, it seemed to me.

There was a mean, rotten part of me that hoped Poppa would be censured, even though it *was* illogical. He deserved to be punished somehow for what he was doing to Rob.

But that didn't happen. Poppa came back before we had finished cleaning up the kitchen and setting the table for breakfast. "It turned out all right," he said. "The council dismissed the charge and gave me a vote of confidence." Momma fixed him a cup of tea, and he settled down with the evening paper. "George Bissell came all the way down from his cabin in the Poconos for the meeting and wound up making an apology. It just goes to show how important it is for all of us to remember how our individual behavior reflects on the entire family. That's something you need to keep in mind, Teddie, now that you're coming along with some rather headstrong notions."

"Yes, Poppa," I said, at that moment not liking my father *at all.*

Grace and her mother came home from the woods on Sunday afternoon. With old Bissell's apology, the ban ended, and Grace was once again allowed to enter our house. We hadn't seen each other for two weeks, since I left for Ocean City.

"What do you think about Julia?" was the first question out of her mouth.

"Julia?" I decided to play dumb. "I think it's just wonderful that she's going to a real finishing school. Now she'll have a chance to practice pouring at teas and curtseying to nobility and so on."

"Oh piffle, Teddie! You don't believe that she's really in a finishing school do you?"

"That's what her mother told me," I said, sticking to my story.

"Of course that's what she's telling people, silly, but my mother found out the truth."

Mrs. Bissell could have wrung truth out of a marble statue, and then she'd tell everyone she could buttonhole. It must have killed her to be up in the woods for a whole week, with nobody to gossip to but squirrels and chipmunks.

"Mrs. Gibbs found out about Tommy, that she was planning to elope with him. And then Julia owned up to the other business," Grace said, lowering her eyes.

"What other business?" I breathed, knowing what was coming.

Grace's eyebrows climbed halfway up her forehead, just the way her mother's did. "You don't know? I thought everybody in town knew that Julia is going to have a baby."

"A baby! Oh."

"Aren't you shocked, Teddie? Don't you think that's the awfullest thing you can imagine? Ma says the worst thing any girl can do is bring disgrace upon her family in this way. Ma says Julia deserves to be punished, though, and her mother, too. Both of them so high-and-mighty, with all their fancy ideas about marrying money."

"I don't think Julia is high-and-mighty, or her

mother either," I said, remembering Mrs. Gibbs's tragic face.

"There must be some reason the boys are always flocking around her," Grace grumbled.

"She's pretty and she's nice, that's why they flock."

"*Nice?*" Grace demanded self-righteously. "You call it *nice*, the mess she's gotten herself into? I'm not going to have anything to do with her if she ever comes back here, which, if she has any shame at all, she won't."

"Grace, how can you feel that way? Julia made a mistake and she's paying for it. She *needs* friends."

"It's more than a mistake," Grace insisted. "It's a sin."

"It's even more of a sin not to forgive somebody."

Mrs. Bissell believed sinfulness was contagious, and now Grace believed it, too. But Grace couldn't help having the mother she did, and she needed a friend, too, to keep her from being completely poisoned. I apologized for saying what I did.

Grace sighed and rubbed her eyes until they were red. Hay fever season had started. "It's so hard when you say one thing and Ma says something else, and both of you sound right."

After dinner Friday Grace and I resumed our Chinese checkers game, this time on my bed. I was winning. Then Rob stuck his head in the door, smelling of bay rum, sang a few bars of "Good Night, Ladies," and trotted down the stairs. It happened so fast that I couldn't tell if his peppy mood was real or not.

"He sure seems jolly," Grace commented. "Is he going out with Babe?"

"I don't know."

If he was, it was probably to tell her he wouldn't be seeing her anymore, just as Poppa had ordered. Then he'd be leaving. I wondered if he'd bother to pretend he was going back to college in a week and a half, or if he was upset enough to leave right away. I was going to have to do something fast. I got so distracted thinking about Rob that I let Grace jump all over me.

"You're worried about Rob. But you really shouldn't be. Everything's going to work out fine."

"Your intuition again?"

"Yes."

"Is it ever wrong?"

"Rarely."

But that didn't make me feel any better.

Saturday morning Rob hunched over the engine of the Chevy, tinkering and tuning. I parked myself on the grass. After a while I said brightly, "I haven't seen Babe lately. How is she?"

"As far as I know, she's fine," he said, frowning at a spark plug.

I wondered if I should remind him that he had seen her last night and should have a more definite report than that. I decided to try a different approach.

"Are you taking her dancing tonight?" I asked, yanking up handfuls of grass. Maybe I'd grab a four-leaf clover and get lucky. "And bringing her here for Sunday dinner?"

Rob scrubbed his hands on the rag that he pulled out of his hip pocket, working around one fingernail at a time. "I'm not taking Babe dancing tonight. And she won't be here for dinner tomorrow."

So I was right. Poppa had ended it. "Why not?" I asked, just to prove it.

"Because I'm going camping with Warren."

"*Warren?* But wouldn't you rather be with Babe? She's terrific! And you really like each other. And Warren is really *dull!*"

"Sure I like Babe. She's a swell gal, but things don't always work out, you know." He squatted on the sidewalk and began lining up his tools like silver spoons in the pockets of the flannel cloth.

"Well, I *know* that, but they *seemed* to be working out. Something happened, didn't it. It was Poppa, wasn't it? I'll bet he told you she's not the right kind of girl for this family. That she's too *flamboyant*. I can tell by your face he said that! But why do you listen to him, Rob? It's your life, not Poppa's! He won't let you be an actor, he won't let you marry the girl you love, he won't let you be what you want to be, and you just stand there and take it! I wouldn't *blame* you if you went out West and got a job!"

Rob stopped tying up his bundle of tools and

stared at me. I tried to think of something to say that would cover up what I had just said. It was too late.

"Out West? Whatever gave you that idea?"

"Oh, I don't know," I said in what I hoped was a nonchalant tone. "It just seemed like an interesting thing to do. Missoula, Montana. Some place like that. Something different from Philadelphia, P.A."

"Well, it would be different, that's true." He sat down on the running board, so that he eyes were level with mine. "But what's this about Missoula? You got a letter from there. Is there something going on that maybe you should tell me?"

I jumped at the chance to escape. "Julia is in love with somebody who has gone to Missoula. That letter was actually for her."

"Oh, I see." He looked relieved. "I was just wondering how you got it into your head that maybe *I* should go out there. Can you keep a secret? Not tell Momma or Grace or anybody?"

"I'm good at secrets," I said.

"To tell you the truth," he said, scuffing at his workboot on the curb, "I had thought about it, sometimes. About leaving here. Maybe going West, like you said."

"Rob, listen! Take me with you!"

This wasn't at all what I had planned to say. I had intended to talk him out of it, but instead I dived in recklessly. "Take me along," I begged. "I don't care *where* we go. I can help. I have some money saved—

almost fifteen dollars. I might even be able to get a job. I'm a good cook now. I could cook on a ranch, for the cowboys. Cornbread. Beans. I can learn to make all that kind of stuff."

Rob's mouth dropped open in an O of surprise, but I tore along without giving him a chance to say anything.

"Maybe Babe could come with us!" I said, getting excited. "There's nothing Poppa could do about *that*. I'll bet Babe could learn to ride a horse, if she doesn't know how already, and she could write about it for a magazine or something. And I could learn to fly! Amelia Earhart used to live in California. That's where she got her start. I could take flying lessons and pay for them with the money I make as a cook."

I got "carried away," as Momma often said I did, and I plunged on. "You were right to make up your mind to go West," I told Rob. "It's impossible here. You can't have any dreams in this family! They'll get used to us not being around, don't worry. Hannah does everything exactly right, just the way they want." I started to cry. "I can't stand it that you're miserable," I wailed, "and I am, too!"

"What makes you think I'm miserable?" Rob asked gently. He moved off the running board and sat on the grass beside me.

"I just know."

"*How* do you know?"

"I'm intuitive."

"Baloney. I have a hunch you're just plain nosy.

I have a hunch you know—or think you know—that I'm miserable the same way you know I had toyed with the idea of going out West. Am I right?"

I nodded. I wanted to die.

"Oh boy," he breathed. For a while Rob didn't say anything, and I didn't either. I just snuffled. "You've read it all?"

"Only the first part."

"What first part?"

"The first month."

"The first month. I see. And may I ask what made you quit at that particular point? Did invading someone's privacy suddenly make you feel guilty? Or did you get bored with it all of a sudden? I'd be curious to know why you stopped, Teddie."

I shrugged. "Because."

"Because *why*?"

"Just because."

"Teddie, this is ridiculous!" Rob exploded.

He hadn't been this upset with me since I was nine and borrowed his Boy Scout knife and lost it— the last time I had touched anything of his until the diary.

"Maybe the real question is, why did you start in the first place? Now look at me and tell me the *truth*, Teddie!"

I tried to look at him, but my eyes kept sliding away. "I found it in your pocket when I was doing the laundry, and I started reading it just to see what it was about. I didn't think you'd really mind, and

I'd find out when you and Peg were going to get married, things like that. But what I found out was that Peg was giving you the air, telling you to go out with other girls and be good but not too good. And you were so miserable you were talking about . . . committing suicide or something . . . and I got scared and kept on reading. And then you said you were going to run away to the West and stay until you forgot her. And then I quit."

"Why did you quit just when it was getting interesting?"

"Because I knew it was wrong. And anyway I could see you were unhappy, but I couldn't do anything about it."

"Well, you did *something*. I presume you're the one who sent the snapshots to Peg?"

"Uh huh."

"And what was the point of *that*, may I ask?"

"They were supposed to be compromising photographs to make her jealous. To show her that she's not the only one who can go out on dates and have a good time."

Rob burst out laughing, but his laughter didn't make me feel any better. "And you haven't looked at it since?"

"Not since I made my vow and wrote it in my diary. I keep one now, too, you know. You can look at it any time you want to."

"It's not much of a diary if you let other people read it," he said. "What vow did you make?"

"That I wouldn't read your diary anymore no matter what, if God would keep you from being so miserable that you'd go out West. And I haven't! Not even when Poppa had that talk with you the other night."

Rob slumped on the grass and shook his head.

"I guess you're pretty mad," I said.

"Well, mad—yes, but that's just part of it."

I kept trying to explain. "The thing is, I thought maybe God had sent you Babe, to make up for Peg, to keep you here. I was afraid you were so mad at Poppa you'd leave for sure."

"What makes you think Poppa broke it up?"

"He didn't? What did he want to talk to you about then?"

Rob jumped up and slammed shut the hood of the car. "For crying out loud, Teddie, will you cut it out? Maybe you'll just have to read the next entry in my diary to find out!"

Warren arrived in time for lunch, naturally. He was the last person in the world I wanted to see. I told Momma I wasn't hungry and stayed in my room until they finished eating and began to pack the car for their camping trip. When at last I crept down to the kitchen to fix myself a huge sandwich, I discovered they needed to do a little more work on the car. Momma found me and sent me out with a big pitcher of ice water and two tin cups.

Warren's long legs stuck out from underneath the

car, the toes of his big shoes pointing east and west. The sight of those clumsy feet made me mad.

Warren crawled out from beneath the car. Sweat grooved the dirt on his face. He wiped it on his sleeve and reached for a cup.

"How's Lady Lindy?" he asked.

"Fine," I said.

"So you really think you could fly an airplane, huh?" he said, holding up the tin cup for a refill.

"Yes." His eyebrows were ginger-colored and spiky, and I didn't like them.

"What makes you think you could do a thing like that?"

"Because I want to, and I *know* I can."

"Takes more than wanting to." *Glug glug.* "Takes brains and guts. Girls don't have that kind of brains and guts. Also takes money." *Glug glug.*

"I happen to have the right kind of brains and guts. Probably a lot more than you do, as a matter of fact. And I'll be able to get the money. Don't worry about that." I *hated* his eyebrows. I hated *him*. He was even worse than Poppa.

"Who in his right mind would put any money behind a girl for such a silly escapade? You might have brains and guts, but you sure don't have much in the way of common sense."

Slosh. I dumped the pitcher of water over his head.

"Go fly a kite, Warren," I said. "Except I don't

think you'd know *how*."

The expression on his face as the water dripped through his ginger-colored eyebrows almost made me smile. Then I turned and ran into the house.

12

Extenuating Circumstances

If Frances had asked me, I would have said no, I didn't want to do it. But when she called, it was Momma who answered the telephone, and she thought it was a lovely idea, to have a farewell-to-summer musicale on Sunday afternoon of Labor Day weekend. If I had continued practicing all summer as I had promised I would, then Frances was sure I could play the Chopin mazurka I had been fooling around with since spring.

Momma assured Frances I'd be glad to play the mazurka, and I'd be right over for a lesson.

I thought it was an awful idea. I had not touched the mazurka in weeks. But I was in so much hot water already in my family—or would be if Rob told them about me dousing Warren with ice water—

that I dug out my music and meekly trotted over to Frances's house.

"It's going to be more of a party than a recital," Frances explained. "Just an informal get-together with refreshments and music-making. Try to think of it as *fun*, Teddie, and maybe you won't be so nervous."

"I'll try." I sat at the upright in the Keelers' parlor, trying to remember to hit the accidental F sharp that cropped up every few measures.

"Have you kept up with your scales and arpeggios?"

"No," I mumbled.

"I really didn't need to ask. But don't worry, Teddie, you'll do just fine anyway. You have a nice feeling for this piece, and nobody ever notices a few wrong notes."

I wanted to ask her if Otis was coming to the musicale, but I didn't dare.

"I was thinking it might be nice if you and Grace would do a couple of duets. I have a few easy pieces that sound more complicated than they really are. You can take them home and try them with Grace, if you want to."

"Okay."

While she shuffled through a stack of music, I was thinking about her and Otis. Rob hadn't said anything about them going out together. She was crazy if she preferred Otis to my brother.

"I was surprised to hear about Julia, weren't you?"

"Yes," I said, wondering which story she had heard.

"Lovely girl."

"Yes." I still didn't know which story.

Frances picked out two pieces from the pile and stuck them in my exercise book. "Have you had a nice time since that lovely dinner? It was such a dear thing for you to do."

"Oh, yes," I lied, a true Schneider.

"That's good." She began making notes on a memo pad for the next lesson. "And how's your family?"

"They're fine. Hannah's going to have another baby."

"Why isn't that wonderful! She and Will must be thrilled."

"I guess so." I gathered up my things to leave and paid her fifty cents for the lesson.

"And Rob?" she asked, sounding very casual and unconcerned. "Is he having a good summer, too? I guess he'll be going back to college soon."

"Right after Labor Day."

"Well, then he'll be around for the musicale. Say hello to him for me, will you? And make sure he knows he's invited?"

"Sure," I promised. At the front door I turned around and said, "Actually, I think Rob's sort of lonesome."

Frances looked surprised and gave a little laugh. "Lonesome? Your brother Robert? Are we talking about the same person? Rob has more friends than anybody I've ever known."

"That doesn't mean he isn't lonesome underneath. You can't judge a book by its cover."

"Well, Teddie, you're right, of course, but I never would have guessed that one. Are you trying to do something about it? Cheer him up or something?" She smiled at me, a sweet, crooked grin. I liked Frances. I wondered if she was still in love with him.

"What about Otis?"

"Otis? What about him?"

"I was going to ask you to call Rob, just to say hello or something," I said. "You know, to cheer him up. But if you're going around with Otis, then I guess that wouldn't be very cheering, would it? Calling Rob, I mean."

Frances sat down on the top porch step and patted the place next to her for me to sit down, too. "Teddie," she said carefully, "what makes you think I'm going around with Otis?"

"Well, he took you home that time," I said, getting hot with embarrassment. "So I just thought you were . . . going around together," I finished weakly.

Frances laughed in her nice way and squeezed my shoulder. "Let's just say Otis isn't my type, and I'm not his."

"You'll call Rob, then?"

"Women don't call men," Frances said. "It's not proper."

"Oh, beans! I get tired of hearing what's proper and what's not. Did you know that I want to be an aviatrix? Nobody thinks that's proper either. They all think I should be a wife and mother and forget about flying. But I'm not going to forget it, no matter what Poppa or that moron Warren, or anybody else says about it. I'm going to be a flier, and that's all there is to it. I think if you want something, then you should try your hardest to get it. If you want to see Rob, I think you should do it. You'll be able to figure out a ladylike plan."

"Teddie, you're really something! You may never become a great pianist, but I don't doubt for a minute that you'll be flying airplanes someday."

A vote of confidence! I wanted to hug her for that, but of course I didn't. Schneiders don't hug. I picked up my music and hurried home, determined to begin working on the mazurka immediately. It was the least I could do for Frances.

I was filled with high resolve. I would do well at this musicale. I would make the family proud of me. I would show them all that Eleanor Louise Schneider was a mature individual, quite capable of taking responsibility for her own life, and not at all interested in meddling in the affairs of others.

I was brisk and efficient in preparing lemon custard to pour over yesterday's pound cake for dessert. Too bad Rob wasn't there to enjoy it, I thought; it was one of his favorites. I washed the dinner dishes with amazing speed, and Momma, who was drying, did not return a single item for redoing.

After dinner I wrote a cheerful letter to Julia, telling her about the forthcoming end-of-summer musicale and the mazurka I would play. I did not include any coded messages.

Then I visited Grace, spoke politely and kindly to her undeserving parents, and proceeded to trounce Grace in two games of Parcheesi, after which I listened sympathetically to a new poem she had written and said praiseful things.

The next morning I fried the Sunday breakfast bacon to crisp perfection and was ready in plenty of time to walk to church with my parents. On the way, Poppa mentioned that his shirt, which I had starched and ironed, was done well.

A breeze, I thought. I had nearly forgotten the sight of water dripping through Warren's ginger-colored eyebrows. Probably Rob wouldn't say anything about it either. I hoped he was having a good time camping.

I even managed to listen attentively to the sermon and was prepared to comment on it during Sunday dinner if the subject came up, as it often did.

But that isn't the way it worked out.

After Poppa had asked the blessing and carved the chicken, Hannah announced in a strong, clear voice, like the president of the women's guild, "Something has to be done about Eleanor." She sounded as though she was discussing a leaky pipe, some practical problem that had to be attended to. "Her behavior has gotten completely out of hand."

"That's strange," Momma said. "I was just about to compliment Teddie on what a young *lady* she's becoming. I think we should be proud of her." She smiled at me. Momma was not the type to notice leaks.

"Mother, you just don't *see* as much as I do," Hannah said impatiently. "You weren't looking out the upstairs window, as I was yesterday morning, in time to see Eleanor hurl a pitcherful of water right in Warren Jennings's face."

Poppa stopped in the act of buttering a slice of bread and laid down his knife. "Is this true, Teddie? Did you throw water at Warren?"

"Yessir," I mumbled, staring at my plate. "But there were *extenuating circumstances,* and he richly deserved it."

"Dear, dear," said Will prissily. "Fancy words to justify an unacceptable action."

"You're a fine one to talk!" I burst out at Will. "And I don't think my behavior is any of your business anyway!"

"Teddie!" Momma gasped.

"*Now* do you see what I mean, Mother?" Hannah demanded smugly. "Completely out of hand."

"You will apologize to Will *at once,*" Poppa ordered.

But I was too mad to stop, now that I had started. "Why do I have to apologize for saying what I think, or for *thinking* what I think? Why should Will sit there and criticize me for what I do? He thinks he's so much better than all the rest of us, and he's just a big windbag!"

Then everybody began talking at once, but Poppa's voice cut through the others. "Go to your room immediately!" he thundered. "And stay there until you are ready to apologize to every one of us!"

I knew they expected me to creep out as meek as a lamb, hanging my head in shame, but I wasn't ashamed; I was furious. I stood up, knees shaking and voice quivering but mouth still in high gear.

"I want to say one more thing before I go. At least I have the courage to speak the truth. And nobody else in this family does. You shut your eyes, you pretend not to see. Has anybody even *noticed* how upset Rob has been this summer, let alone done anything about it? No. You all make believe everything is hunky-dory when it's not. And then when Rob does meet a girl who makes him happy, what happens? Poppa decides she's too flamboyant and tells him he can't see her anymore. *Poppa* decides, and Rob doesn't say a word! But don't you think he doesn't mind, because I know he does! I wouldn't be surprised if he finally just got fed up with all of this and ran way out West or something. And maybe I'd go with him. That would show you. Maybe you'd wake up then." I gulped air and swallowed hard.

"Well, I'm not going to live like that anymore, with everything bottled up inside me until I feel like I'm going to explode. You can punish me all you want, but one of the things I've learned about life is that nobody is going to tell me how I'm going to live mine!"

I glared triumphantly at Poppa. His face was red and his eyes bulged. "Enough!" he roared. "Go!"

I marched with great dignity around the table, up the stairs, and into my room. I shut my door firmly but quietly.

Then I crashed on my bed and cried.

Momma climbed the stairs later in the afternoon and tapped on my door. I didn't answer. I was still curled up on my bed, the counterpane pulled around my head. The knob turned softly and the door opened a crack.

"Teddie?" Momma whispered.

I pretended to be asleep.

She tiptoed in and set something on my nightstand. When she had gone I opened my eyes and sat up. She had left a cup of weak, unsweetened tea and a couple of plain crackers, what she always gave us when we were sick. Momma probably thought I wasn't feeling well.

"Teddie's ill," she must have said to Poppa and the others. "Otherwise she wouldn't have acted like that."

Later she'd insist on taking my temperature, bringing me broth and fruit juice, making me rest, maybe even suggesting a visit to the doctor if I didn't snap out of it fast.

That would be the easy way out—to accept her diagnosis and let her take care of me. But it wouldn't change anything.

I lay there, neither awake nor asleep, for a long time.

Much later I heard the car in the driveway and Rob's and Warren's voices with lots of footsteps and doors opening and closing as they unloaded their camping gear.

There was the clatter of dishes as they got ready for supper. Warren would, of course, be invited to stay, and to the best of my knowledge he had never refused. The thought of food made me hungry. I wondered if someone would bring me something on a tray, or if I would be invited down to face all of them. Poppa had said I had to stay in my room until I was ready to apologize to everyone. That would include Warren.

I'd rather starve, I decided.

"Where's Teddie?" I heard Rob ask when Momma called them to the table, but the answer was muffled.

I was getting hungry. I drank the cold tea and ate the dry crackers and tried not to think about the food on the table downstairs.

The phone rang once while they were still eating. Rob answered. The telephone was on the stair landing near my room, and I could hear clearly his end of the conversation. Someone was inviting him somewhere, and he sounded surprised and pleased. "I'll be over in about a half hour," he said. I thought he might come up to my room then, and I dived under the covers again, determined to ignore him, too. He didn't.

Warren said good-bye to the family, and he and Rob went out together. Hannah and Momma began to wash the dishes in the kitchen directly under my room. I sat by my window and stared out at the garden until it was dark. When I heard Momma's footsteps on the stairs I hurried back to bed and pulled the counterpane around me. This time she left a small tray on the nightstand: consommé, dry toast, and another cup of weak tea. I *would* starve to death at this rate.

I really did fall asleep then, and the loud knock on the door startled me awake. "Who is it?" I called, forgetting that I had made up my mind not to talk to anyone.

"Rob," he said, coming into my room before I could answer. He turned on the bedside lamp. I squinted in the bright light. My clothes were wrinkled and twisted and my hair a mess. Uninvited, he sat down on the edge of my bed. "I brought you a ham-and-cheese sandwich," he say, laying a napkin-wrapped object on my pillow. "I hear," he said, "that when you are not giving shower baths to my friends, you are delivering sermons at the dinner table."

I nodded and reached for the sandwich. He moved it away.

"This isn't the Teddie I used to know. I don't know what to think about you these days."

"Sometimes I don't either," I admitted. "It's just that all of a sudden I've been getting *mad* a lot."

"I'll say! That's an understatement. But what are you so mad at?"

"Well, Warren, for one thing. He had no right to say what he said to me. That I don't have common sense. That I can't fly an airplane because I'm a girl and girls don't have brains and guts and the only thing they're good for is housework."

"He was just teasing you. Couldn't you tell? Actually Warren is very fond of you. He told me so this weekend when we were camping out."

"So how was the camping?" I said, changing the subject.

"Fine. The Perkiomen was running pretty high with all the rain we've been having, but it was good for canoeing. Now, listen—don't change the subject. You can't just go around throwing water on people who say things you don't like, Teddie."

"Why not?" I got up and looked in the mirror and ran a comb through my hair. "I was just teasing, same as he was. How come it's all right for Warren to say whatever he likes to me, but I can't do anything back?"

"It would be better to *say* something. Use words, not water. How's that for a motto?"

"I used words at the table, and now I am *incarcerated*. I should have dumped a pitcher of water on Will, too. That might make it worthwhile being shut up here."

"Yes, but the right words, Teddie, the *right* words!"

"I could have made it like a baptism," I said, picturing how Will would have looked with water dripping onto his black preacher's suit.

Rob smothered a laugh, unsuccessfully. He probably didn't like Will any more than I did, but he'd never say so. "Momma said you're still blaming Poppa because I'm not seeing Babe. And I already told you that wasn't true, but you apparently don't believe me."

"Why didn't it work out, then?"

He shook his head and smiled. "You really have to know everything, don't you? Well, the fact is, Babe is a lot of fun, but we disagree on too many things. She's a high flier—not the kind *you* want to be, though. She has big plans to go to Washington and be a star reporter. I guess when you get right down to it, I'm looking for a quieter type. I don't need Poppa to tell me that."

Rob got up and started pacing around my room, but it was smaller than his room and not arranged for effective pacing. "Poppa is right about a lot of things, you know. He was right about Peg; she *is* too rich for my blood. She wants to marry somebody with money and prestige, and I'll never have much of those. And I know, mad as it makes me to admit it, that he's right about dropping out of Cap and Dagger so I can get my grades up and graduate with a decent class standing. That's what he wanted to talk to me about the other night, by the way; not Babe. Anyway, he's right. I need to be thinking about getting a job next summer. I sure couldn't get anywhere as an actor."

"But you're wrong! You're every bit as good as John Barrymore. You just don't have any confidence in yourself," I protested.

"Well, at least I have one fan."

"I'm not going to let Poppa do to me what he's doing to you," I announced flatly.

"Oh, really? And what is it that he's doing to me?"

"He's ruining your dreams and running your life, whether you're willing to admit that or not."

"Assuming you're right, how do you propose to keep him from doing the same thing to you? He controls the purse strings."

"I don't know."

"I wish you luck, Teddie. But Poppa isn't going to let you be an aviatrix any more than he's letting me be an actor. He'll see to it that you marry the right guy, and you'll end up just like Hannah."

"No," I said. "No."

Rob shrugged. "Incidentally, Frances Keeler called and asked if I'd sing a couple of numbers with her at her farewell-to-summer musicale. I went over to talk to her about it after supper, and we practiced a couple of the duets we used to sing. It was fun. She thinks the world of you, by the way. Frances is a swell gal."

"A peach," I agreed.

"Enjoy your sandwich. I'll see if I can get you some cake and milk, too."

13

A Peculiar Bunch

"Apologize and get it over with," Grace counseled in a loud whisper from beneath my window.

I had now spent two muggy August days in my room going along with Momma's diagnosis of physical illness. In Momma's view, the bad behavior of any of her children could be explained only in terms of germs. But I was now either going to have to show that I actually had some ailment or to stage a recovery. And apologize. Sick or not sick, I still had to apologize.

"All right. I'll do it. I'll come over after dinner and tell you how it went."

Wretchedly is how it went. Making apologies may be easy for some people, but it wasn't for me. The worst of it was that I didn't sincerely regret one word or one drop of water. I'd do it again.

I took a long bath and washed my hair, put on my Sunday dress and a new pair of blue pumps. I went downstairs feeling as though I were going to a funeral. Momma and Hannah were frying liver and onions in the kitchen.

"May I help?" I said.

Momma looked at me carefully and asked, "Are you feeling better, then?"

"Oh, yes. Much."

"Why don't you go out on the porch until we're ready to serve?"

I did as she wanted and sat on the rocker with my hands folded on my lap, waiting for the ordeal to begin.

Hannah asked the blessing, into which she managed to insert a thanksgiving for my recovery and a request that I would continue to "improve."

"Amen!" Will said fervently.

I sneaked a look at Rob, whose lips were twitching back a smile.

"I wish to offer my apologies to everyone in this family," I said solemnly. "Poppa, I apologize. Momma, I apologize." Note that I did *not* say "I'm sorry," because I wasn't. I went around the table, looking each person in the eye and saying the words. Each one acknowledged with a nod except Rob, who said, "It's too bad Warren is missing out on this. Will he get a separate apology?"

"Yes," I said, annoyed that Rob seemed to be enjoying it.

We began to pass the food. When the meat platter reached Will, he sniffed at it and made a disgusted face. "Hannah, what is this stuff, may I ask?"

Hannah said in a small voice, "Liver and onions, Will."

"I thought I made it clear a long time ago that I don't eat liver."

"I'm sorry, Will. I forgot."

"I don't see how anyone could forget a thing like that. I was quite specific about it."

"But that was a long time ago. I didn't know you meant *never*. Poppa likes it so much and we haven't had it in ages. I mean—" There were tears in her eyes. She dabbed at them with a napkin.

Will shoved the offending platter of food toward Momma. "Mother Schneider, perhaps you'd be good enough to take this." He turned to Hannah again. "I don't know what's gotten into you, Hannah. You used to be quite attentive to my needs, but lately it seems you're too preoccupied with other things to remember your duties as a wife. Remember St. Paul's letter to the Ephesians, fifth chapter: 'Wives, submit yourselves unto your own husbands, as unto the Lord. For the husband is head of the wife, even as Christ is head of the church.' "

"You don't love me!" Hannah sobbed.

"Nonsense, Hannah, you're behaving like a child.

I simply detest liver, I don't dislike *you*. Now, go get me a decent meal, there's a good girl."

"I got you a decent meal!" she cried, jumping up from the table. "You're just too st-stubborn to eat it!"

Poppa banged his fist on the table, and the dishes, glasses, and silverware rattled. "What in tarnation is going on around here?" he bellowed. "Can't I have a meal in peace anymore?"

"Shh, Henry. Hannah's not feeling well," Momma said soothingly. "The baby, you know. I'll get you something else, Will. I didn't realize how you felt about liver."

Hannah had run upstairs, and Momma started toward the kitchen.

"Get your own dinner, Will," Rob said.

Momma stopped in her tracks. Poppa stopped with his fork halfway to his mouth.

"I beg your pardon, Robert?" Will said.

"You heard me, Will. Hannah's not your servant, no matter what you think the Bible says. Neither is Momma. Get your own food if you don't like what the rest of us are eating."

Will stammered something unintelligible, his pale hands flailed the air, and he left his place with only a little of his dignity intact.

Momma sat down again. "My word," she said. "What's gotten into everybody, all of a sudden?"

"Blamed if I know," Poppa said. "But if Will isn't

going to eat that liver, pass it down to me. I'll make
sure it doesn't go to waste."

The day of the musicale, Rob persuaded me to
stand out in the backyard, and he snapped a picture
of me with the new Kodak Warren had talked him
into buying. He took pictures of Billy and of Hannah and Will, who had apparently kissed and made
up. When Momma and Poppa came out, Rob had
them pose, and finally Will took a picture of all of
us, including Hannah and Billy. Tinny sat at our
feet.

After the picture-taking we all went over to the
Keelers' house.

Frances had on a rose-colored dress with long,
fluttery sleeves and a deep red sash and a corsage of
white gardenias pinned near her shoulder. "Pretty
as a picture," Poppa said loud enough for everyone
to hear.

Folding chairs had been set up in the parlor, where
the piano was, in the dining room next to it, and in
a separate sitting room where I always waited for my
turn to take a lesson. Grace and I and a half dozen
other pupils were seated in the front row. Most of
us had forgotten that this was supposed to be fun
and were very nervous.

Frances's voice students performed between the
piano numbers. They were pretty terrible, but they
made the pianists sound good. I thought about Julia.

If she had been there she would have sung something beautiful, maybe something from *Madame Butterfly*. I wondered if she was doing any singing in Alabama.

I got through the mazurka well enough. It didn't exactly bring the house down, but everyone clapped politely.

Grace played a Grieg waltz against her will. "I think it's a crime to make people play in a recital who don't like to play at *all*," she said, and as a reward Frances said it would be all right to recite some poetry. Grace read her new poem about a four-leaf clover, each leaf signifying a profound virtue instilled in a child by its parents. She dedicated the poem to her mother and father, who swelled with pride.

Then Frances announced that as a special treat, Rob Schneider was going to entertain us with some popular songs. She sat down at the piano and played a ripply introduction, while Rob took his place next to her, draping one arm casually but elegantly on top of the upright. He sang a couple of numbers from Sigmund Romberg operettas, the kind of music grown-ups like. Poppa was beaming.

Next Rob and Frances sang a duet, "Indian Love Call." Their voices blended perfectly, as though they had been singing together for years. Their second number was "Sympathy," and at the end Frances stood up and they joined hands and bowed to the audience and then to each other. The applause continued, and suddenly Poppa jumped up and called "Bravo!" in a loud voice. The rest of the audience, looking startled but pleased, struggled to their feet, too, and gave Frances and Rob a standing ovation.

A table in the yard was covered with a pink cloth and spread with plates of tiny sandwiches and fancy little pink cakes. There was a large punch bowl filled with something pink and sweet, with a cake of ice floating in it.

Frances circulated among the guests, smiling and accepting compliments. Rob seemed not to be able to take his eyes off her, until he remembered his Kodak and snapped a picture.

After the musicale we all walked home together— except for Rob, who stayed to help Frances clean up. He came in for supper whistling and announced that he would be using the car in the evening. He was taking Frances out for a drive.

Labor Day should have been the most special holiday of the summer.

It was Billy's birthday, and it was also to be the celebration of Momma's August 31st birthday.

There was to be a bridal shower that day for Cousin Marybelle, who had only three and a half months to go until her wedding. Even Earl's parents would be there, the first time any of us would have met them.

It would be a farewell party for Rob, who would be going back to college a week before classes began to organize fraternity rush.

Labor Day was also the last day before I went back to school to begin my sophomore year. I supposed it was better for both Rob and me to be going on with our lives than to be taking off for the West.

The holiday did turn out to be memorable, but not for the reasons I expected.

The first thing that happened was that Will announced they would celebrate Billy's birthday with Will's parents rather than with Hannah's. Billy was the Farquhars' first grandson, too; it was unfair of the Schneiders to monopolize him. We had gone through the same arguments at Thanksgiving, Christmas, New Year's and Easter, and now we had another to argue about. In order to keep peace, Billy would be guest of honor at two parties—at noon at the Farquhars', later on at our house.

They left soon after breakfast, and Momma and I got busy shucking dozens of ears of corn, shaping piles of deviled-crab cakes, mixing up batches of macaroni salad. I made a peach shortcake for Billy's and Momma's birthday, since I still wasn't nearly as talented as Hannah at fancy frosting. That was on the agenda for the following summer, along with yeast breads and doughnuts, and basic dressmaking.

The first guests began to arrive around three o'clock just as the clouds that had been gathering since before noon suddenly let go with a deluge and canceled our plans for a backyard picnic. Aunt Rebecca and Uncle Albert arrived with my cousins Emily, Ferd, and Dickie, all seeming even more babyish than they had on the Fourth of July. Aunt Ida and Uncle Luther did not have to be picked up from the train depot because they had just bought a new car in honor of Cousin Marybelle's impending wedding.

When the rain let up, we all trooped outside to look at the Packard parked behind Uncle Albert's Ford, and while we were admiring it, examining the upholstery and so on—Poppa even crawled into the driver's seat to check the feel of the steering wheel— Earl's Essex zipped around the corner and darted into line behind the other two.

I don't know why I was surprised to see Babe climb out. She was, after all, Earl's sister, and this was a shower for his fianceé. Babe looked like a million in a black dress with a square neckline cut low in front and even lower in back. A long feather swooped down out of her little black hat, and yards of jet beads clicked around her neck.

She took the ebony cigarette holder out of her mouth and kissed Poppa on the cheek as he sat in Uncle Luther's car. She hugged Momma and told me I looked "cute as all get out." Then we all went inside, because it seemed as though it might start to rain again any minute. Earl explained that his parents would be late, having detoured to pick up an elderly aunt.

Momma and I were passing around trays of mint tea and lemonade when the Bissells came over. Grace gawked at Babe, and her parents took on the same squinty look they had when they found us dancing the Charleston. Babe ignored that look, as she usually did anything that smacked of disapproval, and in a matter of minutes was talking animatedly to Mr. Bissell about Lillian Gish's new moving picture.

I was not the only one who had forgotten about Babe. In the middle of one of her stories, Rob strolled in—with Frances.

Babe never missed a syllable, but Rob looked as though he wanted to fall through the floor. Fiddling nervously with the knot of his necktie, he introduced his present girlfriend to his past one.

"Babe, this is my friend, Frances. Frances, Babe here is the sister of Earl over there, who is marrying my cousin Marybelle at Christmas. She's the one with the big blue eyes."

Frances and Babe murmured and nodded to each other pleasantly. Then Rob steered Frances around to the rest of the relatives, some of whom remembered her from the old days.

It was a great performance, among his best, and he managed to keep it up as though he had actually *intended* to have both Babe and Frances there. He even told them both that they had a lot in common because they were fine singers, and then he brought out his ukulele and got them to sing along with him.

Aunt Ida, oblivious to what was going on, was tickled pink to have Frances there to regale with plans for the wedding. While we waited for the rest of the Potters to arrive so that Marybelle could begin to open her shower gifts, Aunt Ida went through her recital again, adding new details: bridesmaids' dresses had been ordered in ruby and emerald velveteen, appropriate to the Christmas season. Aunt Ida begged us to imagine how stunning Babe would look in the dark green with that gorgeous red hair.

"Maybe you'll be lucky enough to catch the bride's bouquet," Frances said, looking innocent.

"Oh, my Lord, I hope not!" Babe said. "I wouldn't touch it with a ten-foot pole. I don't believe in marriage."

"You *don't?*" That was Marybelle's astonished question.

"Heavens, no. I plan to have a career. And I don't think it's possible to do both—have a career and a family—so I'm choosing the career."

"Like Amelia Earhart," I said.

"Who?" asked Aunt Ida.

"Amelia Earhart, the woman flier, the aviatrix. She's almost thirty and she's not married. I think Babe's right," I said boldly. "Career first."

"I believe you'll change your mind someday, Teddie," Frances said. "Marriage and a family are the biggest rewards a woman can have in life. I can't imagine wanting to give them up for a career. I'd never let my music take time away from my husband and children." She fired a challenging look at Babe. "After all, we were created as women to be wives and mothers."

"Created by whom?" Babe asked.

"Why, God, of course."

"I'm convinced she created us to be human be-
ings," Babe said, smiling wickedly.

The "she" sailed by everybody but Marybelle, who
caught it on the fly. " 'She'? What do you mean, 'she'
created us?"

Babe inserted a cigarette in her holder. Rob rushed
forward with a light, but she shook her head and
lighted it herself. "God is a woman, of course," she
said, calmly puffing.

Everybody gasped. It was an interesting debate,
the people *vs.* Babe Potter, but Babe wouldn't back
down. Finally Poppa couldn't stand it anymore, and
he said that foolishness like this convinced him once
and for all that women had no business at all in the
voting booth, *especially* when they decided to vote
Democratic.

Now everybody laughed—except Babe, who
launched into a fiery speech in favor of Alfred E.
Smith for president, insisting that the country was
headed for economic disaster if Hoover got into the
White House.

Aunt Ida appeared deeply shocked. "You didn't
tell me your sister was a Democrat," she said sternly
to Earl.

Earl glared at her. "The whole family is," he said.

Shock waves rippled through the gathering. You
would have thought he had just confessed that the
Potters were horse thieves and cattle rustlers. Marybelle stopped grinning. "You never told me," she

said accusingly.

"The subject never came up, Marybelle, sweetheart," Earl said, trying to pacify her.

"You never told me," Marybelle repeated. "A Democrat."

Earl was getting red in the face. "It's hardly a social disgrace," he said, sounding irritated. "We are all entitled to our political opinions." Then he pointed out that this was in fact Labor Day, a holiday in honor of the laboring man, and the Democratic party was the party of the working class.

"I just can't get over this," Marybelle said, almost in tears. "First I find out you're an Episcopalian, and now a Democrat!"

This remarkable scene ended with Earl stomping out to the Essex, followed by Babe, who was clearly getting a kick out of the whole business. Marybelle was led sobbing to the new Packard by her parents, Uncle Luther shaken out of his lethargy into an angry scowl and Aunt Ida looking distraught at the prospect of her wedding plans going down the drain. Aunt Rebecca and Uncle Albert, seeing that a pall had been cast over the festivities, gathered up Emily, Ferd, and Dickie and left, taking a sackful of deviled-crab cakes with them. Mr. and Mrs. Bissell, probably thinking they had seen all there was to see, went home. Grace stayed.

"Marybelle forgot her shower presents," Momma said.

A stack of unopened gifts were arranged under an

umbrella decorated with crepe-paper streamers and rosebuds on the hall table. Poppa marched over and snapped shut the umbrella, scattering paper flowers.

"Just goes to show it's bad luck to have an umbrella open in the house," he said.

There was a knock at the door.

"Maybe they decided to come back," Momma said hopefully, going to answer it.

A woman with red hair faded to gray and tied with a bright blue headband, and a short, bald man buttoned into a very tight suit clutched the elbows of a tiny old lady dressed in black. The Potters. In their free hands they held pretty packages.

"Sorry we're late," Mr. Potter said, while the little old lady broke away and advanced cautiously over the threshold, feeling her way along with a cane.

"The directions Earl gave us weren't entirely clear," Mrs. Potter added.

Momma rushed forward to help the old lady, who was in danger of tripping over a throw rug. "I'm awfully sorry," Momma said, steering her to a safe spot, "but Earl and Babe and the rest of them have already left. Uh, our niece Marybelle wasn't feeling well."

"Oh dear," Mrs. Potter said. "I hope it isn't anything serious."

"The heat," Poppa said.

"Nerves, most likely," Momma added.

"Prenuptial jitters," Rob threw in for good measure.

"But come on in, folks," Momma said. "Let me get you something cool to drink, and we'll have a nice visit and get acquainted."

"Might as well have something to eat, too," Poppa said, ushering the newcomers into the living room. "Don't want all that food to go to waste."

"Who are all these people?" the old lady croaked, jabbing her cane at us.

Poppa began to pump Mr. Potter's chubby hand. "I'm Henry Schneider," he said, speaking loudly for the old lady's benefit. "My wife, Mamie. My daughter, Teddie. My son, Robert. His friend, Miss Keeler. Our neighbor, Grace Bissell."

One by one we all stepped forward and shook hands.

"Howdya do, howdya do," everybody said.

Momma passed around the iced tea. Everyone sipped politely.

"Ah, well, I think we'll be running along then," Mr. Potter said, setting down his half-empty glass.

"Are you sure we can't offer you some food?"

"Another time," Mrs. Potter said. "Thank you all the same."

They got the old aunt turned around and steered her out the door.

"Thanks for coming," Poppa said.

"Peculiar bunch, ain't they?" the old lady hollered to the Potters as they eased her down the steps.

14

Flight

The peculiar bunch looked at each other.

"Dear, dear, dear," Momma said and began to fan herself with the hanky tucked in the bosom of her dress.

At this moment Hannah and Will and Billy came back from the Farquhars', ready for Part Two of the party.

"Where is everybody?" Will asked.

Hannah looked around at the unopened presents and uneaten food. "What on earth happened?" she wanted to know. Billy, sleeping on her shoulder, stirred and sighed.

"Babe Potter has a wonderful knack for letting skeletons out of the closet," Rob said.

"And the skeletons are all Democrats," Poppa said.

"And Episcopalians," said Momma.

"With the occasional suffragette," Frances added.

"Babe thinks God is a *woman*," Grace said, deeply impressed.

"She wasn't serious?" Hannah demanded.

"May God forgive her her blasphemy," Will intoned.

"Do you think the wedding will go on anyway?" Frances asked.

"*Should* the wedding go on?" Rob asked. "That's the real question."

Hannah laid the sleeping birthday boy on the davenport. "Will somebody *please* tell us what happened here?"

Rob played the whole scene, taking all the parts: Babe saying, "God is a woman, of course," Aunt Ida shrilling, "You didn't tell me your sister was a Democrat," and the deaf aunt's crackling exit line, "Peculiar bunch, ain't they?"

Frances was a good sport, laughing at Rob's falsetto imitation of her proclamation, "After all, we were created as women to be wives and mothers."

"Well, of course we were! I don't see why we're laughing at any of this," Hannah protested.

"What I never got around to saying," Frances put in, "was that I think it's important to use all of our gifts, whatever they may be. Of course I'd always put my family first—but I'd want to keep on with my teaching and playing so long as it didn't interfere."

"My word," Hannah said. At that moment Billy

woke up and started to howl, and Hannah took him out to the kitchen to feed him.

"Well," Rob said, "since the party seems to be over, I was going to suggest that we all take a drive up to the airfield. I hear there's a flying circus in town, and some of the stunt pilots might be performing. Teddie, want to go? Grace?"

A flying circus? *Of course* I wanted to go, but I hadn't even bothered to suggest it. Poppa always disapproved of any activity that took someone away from a family gathering.

"We'll have the birthday cake when you come back," Momma said. "Teddie, better take a sweater with you. That rain really cooled things off."

I ran upstairs to get my favorite fluffy blue sweater. Next to it in the drawer lay the sock full of nickels and dimes, a summer's worth of shirts, pies, darned socks. I scooped out two handfuls of change and dumped it in the pockets of my skirt. The sweater hid the bulges.

We were just climbing into the car—Frances in the front seat next to Rob, Grace and I in back—when who should loom around the corner, whistling "Sweet Georgia Brown" completely off-key, but Warren Jennings.

Grace poked me with her elbow. "Look who's here."

"I'm not blind, Grace."

"Have you apologized yet?"

I shook my head.

Rob invited Warren to go to the airshow with us. I could have killed him. Warren opened the back door and squeezed in. The ginger-colored eyebrows went up when he saw me. "Hello, Teddie. Hello, Grace."

We said hello. The car started off.

"I wish I'd brought my camera," Warren said.

"You can use mine. I've got it right here," Rob said.

"I wish to apologize," I said, staring straight ahead. No answer.

"I wish to apologize," I said again, louder.

"Are you talking to me?"

"Yes!"

"Apologize for what?"

"For throwing water on you."

"Oh, that! Well, that's all right, Teddie. It was a hot day, and anyway, I probably deserved it."

"It was a nasty thing to do, and I'm sorry."

"Not nasty, really," he said thoughtfully. "*Spirited*. I like girls with spirit."

Grace nudged me with her elbow. I rammed her back.

The road to the airfield was crowded with cars, and the grounds were jammed with spectators. Stunt pilots performed barrel rolls and loop-the-loops and dives that made the crowd gasp. Mabel Cody, who was famous for wing-walking, climbed all over a biplane while the pilot put it through terrifying maneuvers. Sometimes I couldn't bear to look.

"Is this what you want to do?" Warren asked me when Mabel Cody's plane landed with her still balanced out on the wing.

"I want to fly commercial planes," I said. "No barnstorming, no stunt flying. Just transporting mail and passengers. Lindbergh says there's a great future for commercial aviation, that someday big planes will fly passengers clear across the country in a matter of hours. That's what I want to do."

"And fly around the world, too," Grace added. "Don't forget to tell him that."

When the aerial stunts were over, the pilots lined their planes up along the edge of the field. For two dollars you could go up for a ride; stunts cost five dollars, according to a signboard set up at the end of the row of planes. I dug my hands in my pockets and weighed the coins. There ought to be enough, I thought.

"Excuse me," I said. "I'll be back in a few minutes."

I walked over to the pilot of a beautiful red plane with white lettering.

"Ride, miss?"

"Yes," I said. "As much time as this will buy, without stunts." I handed him all my change.

My heart pounding, I scrambled into the rear cockpit of the red plane while the pilot counted the money. "Teddie!" I heard Grace's voice exclaim. "Look, she's going to fly!"

The pilot handed me a sheepskin-lined leather

jacket and a pair of goggles and showed me how to strap myself into the seat. Then the pilot climbed into the front cockpit, and his assistant whirled the propeller. A furious roar burst out of the engine, and we began to taxi out to the end of the field. Grace was jumping up and down and waving, Frances was applauding. Warren was *saluting*, for heaven's sake, and Rob was busy taking a picture. I waved grandly.

Some of the other planes with passengers were also getting in line for takeoff. I clutched the bar in front of me with both hands as the plane bumped slowly over the uneven ground and then turned and headed the other way. When it was our turn, the pilot shouted something over his shoulder that I didn't catch. The engine roared, the plane moved off down the field, picking up speed until the nose lifted, the wheels left the ground, and the earth dropped away.

I turned and saw four figures apart from the rest, one with his hands clasped over his head like a champion prizefighter. The figures grew smaller as the ground sank.

The plane leveled off and flew directly north, toward the country where everything was green and gold. After a while the pilot banked lazily to the right, away from the fiery sun on its way toward the horizon, and then headed south, where I caught a glimpse of the hard edges of Philadelphia in the distance.

I don't know how long we flew, how long I had

that exhilarating feeling of freedom and independence from everything that tied me to the earth. But for a while I was part of that engine roar and the lift of the wings. This is it, I thought; this is what I want to do, and I'm going to do it.

The ground rushed up to meet us, and there was a jolt when the wheels touched down. I felt a sudden pull back into reality. We taxied slowly back to the edge of the field, and the four tiny figures grown large again rushed out to meet me. Warren had taken over the camera, and he snapped a picture of me sitting in the cockpit; climbing awkwardly out; standing beside the pilot, who was already looking for other customers.

"All right, who's next?" he asked. "Thrill of a lifetime. One of you folks like a ride?"

"No, thanks," Rob said.

"Teddie's the heroine around here," Warren said. "She's got brains and nerve. And common sense, too." He winked at me. "You'll do it someday. I believe you." I felt myself turn red. I was beginning to hope that Grace might be right.